MW01062442

Ethan

CHRIS KENISTON

USA TODAY BESTSELLING AUTHOR

Indie House Publishing

Indie House Publishing

BOOKS BY CHRIS KENISTON

Aloha Series
Aloha Texas
Almost Paradise
Mai Tai Marriage
Dive Into You
Shell Game
Look of Love
Love by Design
Love Walks In
Waikiki Wedding

Surf's Up Flirts
(Aloha Series Companions)
Shall We Dance
Love on Tap
Head Over Heels
Perfect Match
Just One Kiss
It Had to Be You

Honeymoon Series
Honeymoon for One
Honeymoon for Three

Family Secrets Novels
Champagne Sisterhood
The Homecoming
Hope's Corner

Farraday Country
Adam
Brooks
Connor
Declan
Ethan
Finn
Grace
Hannah
Ian

ACKNOWLEDGEMENTS

Oh boy did Ethan need a lot of help! This is the book where my super fans stepped up and saved the day. Thank you so much to Coral Mitchell for walking me through getting an injured Ethan from the sandbox to Texas and Jessie Collins for helping me break Ethan's ankle LOL. You guys saved my last minute sanity! My dear friend Jan from San Diego once again came through with legal pitfalls to avoid, and my big brother Chris walked me through the quandaries of criminal law. You both rock! Of all the Farradays so far, Ethan has been the hardest brother to write, and perhaps as a result the one my team is the most proud of. I hope you enjoy Ethan and stick around for the rest of the family to come. Did I mention cousin Hannah will be in Tuckers Bluff soon?

Yeehaw and enjoy!

Chris

CHAPTER ONE

"Clear to lift."

Weeks of planning, coordinating, and training until the team could have executed this mission in their sleep was about to pay off. Eight souls aboard and another pilot on their way home.

Out of nowhere shouts of *"missile, missile, missile!"* sounded in Ethan's headphones. Over his shoulder he caught the signature of the ground-to-air-missile. *Damn.* A kaleidoscope of orange and yellow flashed to his right as the helicopter rocked left. *Son of a...* The aircraft pitched up and down, then side to side. Not how he'd planned to end this mission. Using the intercom, he called for the other pilot to empty his weapons system. *"Fire it out."* Making a spiral descent, this bird was going down. Fast. *Crap.*

Surrounded by difficult terrain, the GPS, radio and emergency beacon probably wouldn't be worth a damn, and time was not on his side. Riding a pissed off bull with his nuts strapped was a piece of cake compared to controlling a helo with its tail boom severed. He had nine men on board. They'd come too damn far not to make it back to their families. *You go home with the one that brung ya.* Today was not a good day for these men to die. Ethan had brought 'em and he was taking 'em home.

The pounding repetition of gunfire blanketed them like the constant static crackling of a struggling comm system. Smoke seeped into the cockpit and the mountainside grew too damn close. "Not today," he muttered. Flames licked at his aircraft like a lizard trapping its prey. "Brace for impact!"

Ethan's eyes sprang open. *Breathe. Calm.* He was alive and... *not* hanging upside down. Blinking hard he glanced down at his hand. No shrapnel, no blood. A bandage. He blinked again and swallowed a hard gulp of calming air. "The men," he muttered before he remembered what was left of the helo had gotten all his passengers on the ground in mostly one piece.

"Are fine, Major." A tall attractive woman crossed the short distance from the doorway to the bath and emerged with a washcloth. Not saying a word, she dabbed away the sweat that had settled over his brow and trickled down his face.

Her name was on the tip of his tongue. He knew this woman, but his mind was still half asleep and the other half was back in the sandbox.

"I'm told what you did was nothing short of miraculous. Not many people survive helicopter crashes—"

"Controlled hard landing." He didn't want to hear the word crash again.

"Sorry. As I was saying, not many survive a hard landing, never mind an entire crew."

Now he remembered. Commander Billings. His surgeon. They must have put him back on some of the stronger meds. He hated the drug-induced brain fog. "How fine is fine?"

The pretty doctor frowned and then smiled again. "The other pilot is already patched up and back with your unit."

The fog in Ethan's brain continued to lift. He knew that. Knew his buddy Hammer was okay.

"The majority of the team are recovering from a range of broken bones, minor concussions and lacerations. A few first degree burns from getting everyone to safety. Lieutenant Bishop had to undergo surgery for a ruptured spleen along with a lacerated liver, but he's recovering nicely."

Ethan knew that too. "You already told me this, didn't you?"

The commander nodded. His forgetfulness must have been what had her frowning before, now she seemed pleased to have him remember. "You're progressing well. Foot looks good. Your hand too."

He wiggled his fingers and his toes. He wasn't sure how many days he'd been here, but he did know he was ready to get off his back. "How long before I return to duty?"

A single brow arched high on her forehead. "Marines," she muttered, softly shaking her head. "That's a serious break. You've had multiple surgeries and a nasty infection with a high fever that has kept you mostly asleep for the better part of a week. Your bones will need the same six to eight weeks to heal as those of mere mortal men."

Something about the way she teased made him relax. Reminded him of home. Now he remembered. He'd been looking at the computer, catching up, when he couldn't stay awake any longer. How long ago was that? "My family?"

"Yes, well. It seems there was a bit of a paper glitch."

"Glitch?"

"They only received official notice of your status yesterday. I understand your father and brother are on their way."

"No." If the doc was planning on keeping him on medical orders for two months, that meant he'd be going back to home station when released. In that case he might as well use up his accumulated leave and get his ass home. If he had to be laid up he'd rather do it on the ranch. Not that going back to Pendleton was a bad thing—it just wasn't home. "That's not necessary."

"The hell it's not." Sean Farraday strode into the room. Over six foot, dressed in standard West Texas attire of jeans, button down shirt, first place rodeo buckle, well worn—and polished— boots, and of course, his Stetson, the man was an imposing presence. And a bit of an anomaly in Washington D.C. "You're just lucky Aunt Eileen isn't here or she'd be hugging the stuffing out of you already."

Ethan began to chuckle and a pulling pain stabbed at his side.

"Bruised ribs," the doctor explained. He didn't remember that. Of course, he hadn't had anything to laugh about since arriving at Walter Reed. "I'm Commander Billings," she said as she extended her hand.

"How do you do?" His dad, having removed his hat, shook the offered hand. "You been taking good care of my boy?"

The woman's eyes twinkled with humor, but she had the decency not to laugh at Ethan being referred to as a boy. "We're all doing our best."

"Good." His father turned, a crease between his brow, and approached his son. "How ya feeling, really?"

"Like a swim in the creek. Should be nice and high about now."

His dad smiled. "Could be better."

"Not enough rain?" The brain fog hadn't lifted. He should know the answer.

"Enough," Sean answered, studying his son from head to toe as if he were a brand spanking newborn.

"So what's the other guy look like?" Slipping a phone into his pocket, his brother DJ came into the room and stuck his hand out at the doctor who seemed a bit awestruck at a second six-foot-plus man in cowboy hat and boots. "I'm Declan."

"Declan?" Ethan muttered in surprise. "You in the doghouse?"

His dad shook his head, smiling. "Seems Becky thinks Declan is a nice name."

So he wasn't misinterpreting the internet posts. "I'll be…"

"If you'll excuse me." Dr. Billings stepped aside. "I have rounds to make. If you have any questions the nurse can page me, otherwise, if he continues to show improvement, your son should be on his way back to California within the week."

DJ and their father exchanged a quick sideways glance and Ethan didn't like the look of it. Somewhere between the post surgery haze and the high fever, he'd discovered the barrage of contacts from his siblings and wondered what was up. Slowly the pieces in his mind were falling back into place. Once he'd seen the doe-eyed photos of his brother and Becky, he'd figured that's what the messages were all about. The Farraday brothers were dropping like flies. At least he knew for sure not only was Becky a great catch, but he would kick his brother's sorry ass from here to Bagram if he let her down. But that look on his father's face seemed to have nothing to do with lovesick sons.

"So what the hell is going on?"

• • • •

Hot water pounding on her back, Allison Monroe swore there wasn't a blessed thing better in life than running water. If she had to choose between a toilet and a water heater, a hot shower would win every time.

Tomorrow morning she'd report to the small office base for MHI, Mobile Healthcare International, and catch up on the happenings in the civilized world, but until then she had a date with a very warm and comfortable mattress. After living on either a boat or in tents in very remote villages for the last seven months, a real bed came in second place after a hot shower, nudging the toilet easily into third place. Sleeping past sunrise was a long awaited luxury.

The one aspect of even small-city life she was not looking forward to was the ritual of primping and fussing with hair and makeup before facing the public. Wet hair twisted in a towel on her head, and smothered in a terry cloth robe, Allison sank onto the feathery bed and reached for her laptop. At only seven o'clock, if she let herself fall asleep now she'd be awake long before sunrise.

"Some of the crap." This is why she spent seven months every year away from civilization. The things people felt compelled to complain about on social media as though they were life and death. "I want to see you up to your knees in sick and dying children and then tell me how important it is that your city councilman not be allowed to promote his alma mater. Really."

Shoving off the mattress, Allison unwrapped the towel and shook her hair out. Not even in the tropical heat did her hair fall anything but pin straight. Tossing the towel into the bathroom, she crossed the room and grabbed a mango. This she was going to miss. Especially the native fruits that couldn't be found even in the lush northern California valleys. And the friendly service. Most days when people went out of their way to help *la doctora*, she felt more like a queen than a physician.

A few *ciduelas* in hand, the small red and orange fruit having nothing in common with American plums, and a small dish with the mango she'd sliced, Allison plopped herself in front of the laptop again. "Maybe email won't be so bad." Deleting all the unsolicited correspondence from the multitude of African princes wishing to gift her millions of dollars and the seminars on how to become a real estate mogul with an empty bank account and a few other physiologically improbable advertisements, Allison focused on emails from people she actually knew.

Most of her friends understood that while traveling from village to remote village south of the equator, finding a Wi-Fi hot spot would be as likely as discovering the fountain of youth. Others not so much. Which left her with a long list of apologies to send for missing the barbecues, birthdays, and other celebratory events of her coworkers in recent months.

"Meredith?" The email from her landlady popped out at her. Meredith was most certainly one of the people who would know better than to think Allison would get email.

Not sure when you'll see this, I left a message on your cell too. Strangest thing, had a visit from some guy from Brooklyn Security and Investigations in Miami looking for you. Well, actually he was looking for your sister. I told him he had to be mistaken, that you don't have a sister, but he was rather persistent.

"Oh, Francine. Now what?" Allison's chest constricted, the same breathless pressure she felt whenever circumstances had her thinking about the sister who'd taken a path so different from her own. For as long as Allison could remember, her sister had been in one disastrous mess after another. At first with their poor aunt who hadn't a clue what to do with her, then with her teachers, and with the police, until one day she was just gone. Once in a while Allison would receive a postcard, like the time Francine got married. Then divorced. And still another declaring her path to stardom now that she'd become a model. All the cards postmarked from California had been the catalyst to Allison accepting a scholarship to Stanford. Even though at the time, Allison never had a clue where her sister was, or what shenanigans she was up to, somehow she'd felt better knowing they might at least be in the same state.

He left his card and I didn't think anything more about it until Mark mentioned the same investigator showed up at the hospital looking for you there too. The guy insists it's important he find your sister. Just in case you want to reach him as soon as you have access I've attached a scan of the card with all his contact info.

Allison clicked on the attachment. Plain card. Nothing fancy. Straight and to the point. Probably some kind of hoax or gimmick like the foreign royalty scams. She closed the file and returned to her email. Five or six emails down the list and she didn't have a clue what she'd just read. What if the investigator wasn't a scam? What if something had finally happened to Francine? No, that didn't make sense, if the guy was looking for her then he wouldn't know if something was wrong. Or would he? "Blast."

Switching over to the email Meredith had sent, Allison scribbled the number onto the pad by the bedside table then sprang to her feet and dug out the cellphone, still in its plastic bag. Tucked away deep in her suitcase, she hadn't expected to use the phone until she was on her way home in another week or two. If she was going on a wild goose chase, at least she had a decent international phone plan. Tapping in the digits from the circled phone number, Allison waited impatiently through each ring.

"Brooklyn Security," a deep voice with a hint of New York answered.

"Yes," she cleared her throat, "this is Allison Monroe. I understand someone from your office is looking for me."

The sound of keys clacking echoed in her ear before the voice responded. "Oh yes, we were hoping you might have been in contact with your sister, Francine, recently."

Clearly the guy wasn't very good at his job or he'd know that Allison had been in the South American jungle for the last seven months.

"Any time within the last year," he clarified.

"No." That was easy enough. Allison hadn't heard from her sister since she needed bail money well over a year ago. Francine had insisted the drugs weren't hers. Allison desperately wanted to believe her, but by the time she'd hopped a flight to San Diego, Francine had disappeared. Again. The phone number not working and the woman at the address her sister had given her claimed she hadn't seen Francine in well over six months. It amazed Allison that in this day and time it could be so easy for someone to live off the grid. She just hoped it didn't mean her big sister was on the streets. That thought scared the crap out of Allison almost as much as nightmares of drug dens and DWI crashes.

"It's rather important my client speak to Francine. When was the last time you saw your sister?"

"The day after her sixteenth birthday." Allison squeezed her eyes shut. The fight between Francine and their Aunt Millicent had been the worst since they'd moved in with her.

"Spoken with her?" he asked.

Whenever she needed money in a hurry.

"Dr. Monroe?"

"Over a year ago." She wasn't sure why she answered him. Somewhere deep inside maybe she was hoping this man could do what none of the investigators her Aunt Millicent had hired could.

"Possession charges." It wasn't a question. Allison nodded. For all the good that did the guy on the other end. Not that he seemed to need her affirmation. "And she hasn't made any attempt at contacting you in the last few months?"

Allison shook her head. "Not that I know of, I'm still out of the country."

"I see. When will you be returning to the United States?"

"Maybe you should tell me why you're asking all these questions about my sister?" Silence hung heavily on the other end as more keys clacked in the background and Allison held her breath. She didn't like the feel of this.

"Dr. Monroe, are you aware that you have an infant niece?"

"A what?" There had to be some mistake. This man had to be looking for a different Francine Langdon, or whatever name she went by now.

"Your sister left an infant girl on my client's doorstep. I've been hired to locate Francine now that paternity has been established."

Paternity? Allison was on her feet and throwing things back into her bags. Tomorrow's meeting with the other mobile clinic team leaders for a plan of action for the next round of doctors willing to brave the Amazon jungle was about to become the shortest session in MHI history. Sooner, rather than later, she would be on a plane heading stateside to… she froze mid toss, "Where exactly did my sister leave my niece?"

• • • •

Stunned didn't begin to describe the feelings coursing through Ethan's veins like an IV push. He'd faced irate superiors, belligerent recruits, crazed insurgents, and death, but nothing left him as paralyzed as the thought of fatherhood. "You're sure?"

DJ and his father nodded in synchronized unity.

Of course they did. They'd already told him about the DNA tests. Even if his DNA hadn't been tested, why would any woman who might have slept with one of his brothers go all the way to California to deliver a baby just to bring her back to Texas and pass her off as Ethan's? He looked at the birth certificate in his hand. Francine Langdon. Why didn't that ring a bell? Yeah he liked women, and yes, like most men on leave he enjoyed their company, but it wasn't like he was banging a harem at every opportunity.

No strings, no commitments was SOP. Military pilots made lousy husbands. Most women knew that. At least the ones he'd been with. But damn it, even so he'd always been a gentleman. Always knew the lady's name, what she liked, and always made sure they parted ways on a good note feeling a hell of a lot better than when they'd met.

"Francine," he repeated softly.

The brow over DJ's left eye arched high on his forehead and Ethan knew he'd been busted.

"There was a letter with the birth certificate," DJ said equally softly.

Their father turned his head to look at DJ, a momentary glint of surprise in his eyes.

DJ hefted one shoulder at his dad and then turned to Ethan. "She signed it Fancy."

Fancy. He'd known all along that couldn't be her real name, but she'd never told him anything more. It had been a very long weekend after an extensive and grueling training assignment. All he'd wanted was a few beers, a couple of games of pool, and chance to think of nothing at all, especially the reason for all the training.

She'd come off a break-up with a guy she'd not so affectionately dubbed the King of Asses. One time too many she'd almost done jail time because of the loser's drug habit and she'd finally smartened up and walked away. He'd been under the impression that going it alone had been hard on her. He remembered the night well.

A strawberry blonde with dazzling blue eyes and a southern California tan. Fancy looked a bit too happy when she'd first walked into the bar, as though this hadn't been her first stop, but she could walk a straight line and had a friend at her side. An hour later the friend was nowhere to be found and a squid who'd drunk his own weight in Tequila had his hands all over her. Ten minutes later Ethan was almost out the door when he did a last look over his shoulder. Sure enough, octopus hands was getting more friendly, but this time the blonde strained to pull away.

Ethan wasn't about to stop a legal-age woman from having a good time if that's what she wanted, but there were rules that every decent man followed, even those who had been in the sandbox for a hell of too long a time. No means no, and yes on the heels of too much booze didn't count.

It didn't take more than a few additional seconds to realize, whatever this lady might have said before, she'd had a change of heart now. In a few long strides, he'd crossed the floor and drew to a stop beside the blonde. She was even prettier up close and definitely had crossed the ethical limit for consent. "Sorry I'm late," he said with his best smile.

Eyes wide open, the blonde looked over her shoulder, a flash of fear streaking in her gaze. The buffoon shackling her arms in his beefy grip merely growled.

"You ready for a ride home?" Ethan asked, ignoring the daggers aimed at him by the guy who could see his chance at getting lucky slipping away.

"I, uh." She blinked and looked at him again. Her gaze shot over to the other guy, then quickly turning back to Ethan, she nodded.

Carefully, he eased his hand around her forearm. "Let's go."

Immediately her gaze dropped to his hand and at the same moment, the tension in her body eased. Maybe it was the fact that he'd barely touched her rather than manhandled her like a horny gorilla, or maybe it was just an instinctual thing recognizing he meant her no harm. Either way, she smiled up at him. "Let's."

None too happy about the change in plans, the idiot squid lunged at Ethan and it hadn't taken more than a couple of swings to lay the drunk out cold. A couple of Benjamin Franklins on the bar for the inconvenience and they'd escaped to the parking lot before an all-out Marines vs. Navy brawl exploded.

"You still with us?" his father asked.

Ethan nodded. He felt numb, and not from the painkillers. "I'll get leave."

"The doctor said you could be here another week."

"Doesn't matter."

"Oh yes it does," his father said. "You're not going to do anyone any good if you don't heal right."

"I've got medical orders. I'm supposed to return to Pendleton.

Follow-up treatment then therapy."

"When are you due back on base?" DJ asked.

Ethan shook his head. "Soon. I'll talk to my CO. I've got leave coming. No reason I can't do my waiting for therapy time from home." *Home.* He wiggled his toes and realized he wasn't so worried about his ankle anymore. He had something way more important to figure out.

CHAPTER TWO

The week from hell might just be coming to an end. A good end. At least that's what Allison prayed for. Getting any more information from one Luke Brooklyn Chapman over the phone had been impossible. He did, however, take the time to reassure her that her niece could not be in better care. She wasn't all too sure how good a judge of that he was, but a few minutes on Google told her the former Navy SEAL probably understood human nature better than she did. The only other thing he'd agreed on was to speak to his client and get back to Allison. However long it took for him to call back, it wouldn't be soon enough.

Not that she could do anything with the information even if the man had turned the call around right away. Despite her best intentions, walking out on the MHI didn't prove to be easy. Changes, challenges, a society that functions at the pace of an aged tortoise, and one very sick surgeon kept Allison in country an entire week more than she'd wanted. Then considering there was no such thing as a direct flight from the Amazon jungle to San Francisco, making her way home took days. With only one flight a day out of the small isolated town, like it or not, it took Allison two days and two flights just to get to the capital. Too late for the morning flight out of the country meant a third day until she'd take off for Miami. Storms all along the Eastern Seaboard conspired against her, stranding the aircraft intended to transport her to Dallas at its point of origin. With a bazillion travelers all rearranging their flight plans, days four and five passed before luck turned her way in Dallas when she got the last seat on the last flight to San Francisco.

Finally home, almost two weeks after the world-altering phone call and dead on her feet, playing telephone tag with

Brooklyn and her new lawyer had been another thorn in her side. Unwilling to sit and do nothing, she'd unpacked, tossed in a load of wash, and first thing in the morning she'd packed up again and driven down to San Diego. The last place she'd known her sister to be. Or at least for her, the last people she was aware of who even knew her sister and likely her only chance to get at the truth.

Now, stuck in bumper-to-bumper traffic doing fifty-five miles an hour, her phone rang and the security company's name appeared in front of her. *Finally.*

"Any news on my sister?" No point in wasting time on polite how-do-you-dos.

"Wherever she is, she doesn't want to be found. Traditional means of tracking aren't working. She doesn't use credit cards."

Hard to have credit cards without credit.

"No cellphone accounts and hasn't filed a tax return in over five years," he continued.

Honestly, Allison was a bit surprised her sister had *ever* filed a tax return. "What about my niece?"

"I have an investigator in your area still, I'd prefer any exchange of information be in person."

Well, at least the guy was careful. Not that doctors working overseas were clamoring to impersonate her and steal a child, but still. On the other hand, nothing in that statement revealed if he intended to tell her where to find Francine's little girl. "I'm not home. I'm in San Diego."

"Really?" She could hear the surprise in his voice.

"Really." For no apparent reason the traffic cleared in front of her and she stepped on the gas. The exit to her sister's last known place of residence was only a few miles down the highway. "I don't want to put this off any longer."

"Agreed."

"Really?"

The man on the other end of the line laughed. "Don't sound so surprised."

It was a nice laugh and for the first time she felt like maybe she wasn't in this fight alone. "Sorry."

"I'll text you the number of my guy near LA, maybe he can drive down and meet with you. When you're at a stopping point, give him a call. He'll want to see some ID, but he'll tell you everything you want to know."

"Thank you." A few more hours at most and she'd know where her niece was, and if her luck was changing, maybe she'd even have a lead on her sister.

"I meant what I said the last time we spoke. Brittany really is in excellent hands. You don't need to worry."

Don't worry? He might as well have told her not to breathe. Not until she could bring Fancy's daughter back to San Francisco would Allison even begin to relax. Drawing the call to an end, she pulled off the exit and followed the GPS to the last known address she had for her sister. By the time she'd found a parking spot she'd also spoken with Brooklyn's investigator. Turns out he was in San Diego on some other business and could meet her in thirty minutes. Instead of heading up the stairs to knock on the door, she opted to wait for him at the park across the street. Strategically placed as though put there specifically to give her a direct view of the building, an empty bench called to her.

Working all day in portable tents in hot and humid temperatures with bugs and sounds suitable for a cheap horror flick only to pack up and move down river and do it all over again was exhausting. Yet not once in her seven months did she feel as bone weary as she did from hurrying only to sit here and wait.

At first she kept her gaze on the building across the way and the occasional person moving along the sidewalk. The odds of her sister being one of them were infinitesimal. That was if Allison even recognized her sister. More years had passed living without Francine than living with her. The thought sent chills down Allison's spine and had the hairs on her arms standing on edge.

Rubbing away the chill, she felt a heavy weight drop in her lap. Looking down, Allison saw she was the recipient of a very wet and well-chewed baseball. The deliveryman? A rather shaggy four-footed pup with a lolling tongue sticking out from what looked like a happy grin.

Picking the sodden ball up with two fingers, she scratched his ears with the other hand. "I'm guessing you want to play fetch?"

The dog woofed and lifted a paw. "Okay, you win the cute award for the day." She gave him another scratch and looked around for his owner. Several yards away a man sat on another bench glancing in her general direction. "Is that your person?"

The dog nudged her hand.

"Okay. I get it. Throw now, talk later." Ignoring the slobber, she raised her arm and hurled the ball as far as she could.

The furry mutt took off at a full gallop, and, ball in mouth, trotted to the man at the other bench. The man laughed and rubbed his hand down the animal's back. "I guess that's your person." She watched another moment as the man tossed the ball with way more force than she had, before returning her attention to her phone.

The clock was ticking slowly. Or maybe waiting on an investigator to answer all your burning questions was the same as watching a pot of water not boil. Perhaps if she watched the man and his dog playing catch... Even at this distance he was easy on the eyes. And had a good arm. She wished she could hear his laugh. And wasn't that just ridiculous. In a few hours she'd be back on the road home and the guy and his dog would be long gone. Probably home to a wife and kids.

And what difference did that make? She wasn't in the market for a new man, especially not one hanging out in a park in the middle of the afternoon. No, what she needed was to find out what kind of crazy mess Francine had gotten into now.

• • • •

Ethan would kill for a recliner. He'd tried stretching his bad leg out on the bench. It had worked for a short while. He'd used a wheelchair all week at Pendleton to haul himself all over the base filling out papers and securing leave. Only now, his first day approved for crutches, and it wasn't the hand the doctor was so concerned with that gave him trouble, it was his leg that throbbed and his foot had once again swollen to abnormal proportions. Nothing short of an upended cloud would ease the pain.

With hours to kill until his flight to Texas, waiting here in hopes of seeing Fancy was probably not the smartest thing he'd ever done, but hanging around the base or the airport wouldn't accomplish anything either. He was actually a little surprised he so easily remembered the way to the last place he'd seen her.

It certainly had been one hell of a few days. Not until he was pulling out of the bar parking lot with a very tipsy passenger did he realize the blonde beauty had nowhere to go. At first he'd thought she was simply too drunk to remember but too soon he realized her memory wasn't the problem. Two hours and several cups of coffee later he'd heard the entire story of the jackass she'd lived with, listened to her leave a multitude of messages with friends in search of a place to crash. Finally, he concluded the only way either of them would get any sleep tonight was if she came home with him. It wouldn't be the first time he'd given up a comfortable bed and crashed on a sofa, and most likely wouldn't be the last.

He'd awoken the next morning to the smell of bacon sizzling and coffee brewing. Not a bad reward for sleeping on the too short couch. By the end of the day most of her friends had responded with one reason or other why she couldn't crash at their place. Ethan had a feeling most weren't very good friends at all, and he'd done his best to distract her disappointment with a whirlwind day of So-Cal tourism. The day of fun and frolic had continued into the night—and his bed. The next day one friend had extended Fancy a lifeline, but somehow she'd spent another two nights with him before he'd brought her here.

A furry mutt that looked like an awkward mix between several breeds ranging from husky to shepherd to something with silky fur sat at his side and nudged his hand.

"Where did you come from, fella?"

The dog dropped a slobbery ball in his open palm and

reflexively Ethan tossed it into the open field. At least playing with the mutt would make the time pass a little faster waiting for Fancy's friend to show up. Except instead of bringing the ball back to him, the friendly canine trotted off to greener pastures. So intent on the apartment across the street and the wheels churning in his own mind, Ethan hadn't even noticed when the woman and her dog had arrived.

A car door slammed and Ethan shot his attention across the street to the little red car. A big hulking guy, the driver clearly wasn't Fancy's friend.

A weight fell into his lap and the same dog sat back on his haunches. Instead of a baseball, Ethan stared at a white bag from a burger joint. "Sharing your lunch?"

"I'm afraid that would be mine." A breathless voice called to him. The dog's owner came trotting up beside him. "Unless you like avocado bacon turkey burgers."

"Thank you, but I'm more of a steak and potatoes man." Forgetting about his injured leg, he instinctively went to stand and groaned at the pain shooting from toe to hip.

"Oh, please. Don't get up." The woman's gaze danced from his foot to the crutches at his side and back to his foot. The cursory glance turned more serious. "You really should have that leg elevated above your heart."

"Yes. Nurse?"

"Doctor."

Ethan winced. "Ouch."

"Seriously, you need to at least lean it up on the bench here."

"No. I mean my aunt would have my hide for making such a stupid presumption. My sister the lawyer would be in line behind her."

The lady had a very pretty smile and a sweeter laugh. "Apology accepted. But you really—"

"Should get the leg elevated. Yes. I'm just killing time until I have to catch a plane tonight. When I get home that same aunt is going to make damn—excuse me—darn sure that I follow doctor's orders to the letter."

"I like your aunt. So will your doctor. But if you're going to be flying with that leg you should make sure to hydrate well and it won't hurt to take some aspirin or ibuprofen now and again before catching the flight. Thrombosis is a risk for anyone when flying, worse for someone in your condition."

"Yes, ma'am." Ethan nodded. His doctor had told him exactly the same thing. Before he could say another word he spied the man from the red car standing several yards away, scanning the park.

The pretty brunette followed his gaze and spotted the man. "Oh, I think that's who I'm waiting for." She grabbed the white bag. "Take care of that leg."

Ethan nodded again and watched her back as she hurried toward the man, the dog trotting at her heels. "Lucky guy."

Another door slammed, and once again Ethan turned his attention to the street. A gangly teen exited the car, and siphoned the air from Ethan's lungs. It wasn't like he'd really expected this rudimentary stake-out to be profitable, and yet, disappointment coursed through him. Which begged a new question—what the hell would he do if the next person to step out of a car actually was Fancy?

CHAPTER THREE

The uncomfortable flight into Dallas/Fort Worth International Airport might as well have been a boxcar on a freight train. With seats unsuitable for the average mature adult, comfort was not an option. The bulkhead seating with extra leg room was the only bright spot to the trip home. Though Ethan couldn't completely elevate his foot, the flight attendant had been kind enough to bring some pillows and a blanket from first class to create a hassock of sorts that eased some of the throbbing from swinging himself about all day on crutches.

Behind the wheel of her car, his sister Grace glanced his way. "How's the leg holding up?"

"Fine." Dozing in the front seat of her car hadn't done much to ease the pain, but he wasn't about to say the damn thing hurt like a son of a... "Just fine."

"Glad you got some rest. We're almost home. I have a feeling things are going to be hopping."

Hanging out at the airport to catch a commuter flight to Abilene or Lubbock only to still have to drive all the way to the ranch would have taken more time and been harder on his leg than the insanely long drive from Dallas to Tuckers Bluff. "You didn't have to do this. I could have rented a car."

"Oh yeah. I can see Dad and Aunt Eileen agreeing to that one." Grace chuckled, shaking her head. "The timing was great. I've got a short break before my classes start again. It makes more sense for me to make the trip home rather than Finn or Dad making the drive roundtrip."

He wasn't going to argue. Truth be told, he was damn glad to have a family that cared about him this much. Straightening in his seat and looking around he realized they were indeed practically spitting distance to the ranch. "The least I could have done was stay awake and keep you company."

His sister smiled at him again. Even as a baby Grace smiled at almost everything. Of course, most of the time she'd get that gleam in her eye that warned everyone she was up to something. As the youngest of the family and the only girl it hadn't mattered much, she was spoiled rotten.

"I actually like the peace and quiet," she continued. "It's a nice break from the normal hustle and bustle. For a little while anyhow." That twinkle appeared in her eye as her smile tilted a little higher to one side. "Besides, I am sooo ready to meet the new girl in the Farraday clan." She turned her head to face him. "It wasn't easy growing up the only girl with you bunch."

Easy for who? Ethan almost laughed, but he just didn't seem to have it in him. He wished he didn't still feel quite so numb all over. Since he'd first been told about his recent fatherhood he was having a hard time feeling anything. Wasn't a man supposed to be overjoyed by a child? Or was that only when the child belonged to the love of your life? Once he'd gotten over being stunned, he'd felt almost hollow. Neither love nor hate. The idea scared him. Had being in the drudges of the sandbox robbed him of the depth of human emotion? He forced his mind back to his last visit home. To Adam and Meg's wedding. The smiles. The joy. The love. His heart had been full at the happiness streaming from his older sibling. Yes, he could still feel some things.

"What?" Grace shot a quick glance in his direction. "No warning not to spoil the little peanut?"

"Peanut?"

"Well, that's not very girly but it sounded better than pumpkin or pipsqueak. I'm sure once I see her in person something more appropriate will come to me."

"How about Brittany? It's her name."

"Yeah." Grace frowned. "Would have been cool if she'd been Heather or Hailey or—"

"We've already got an H in the family. Hannah."

"Yes, I know. And it was very thoughtful of Aunt Anne to honor Mom by picking up the next letter after G, but still. Maybe Helen would have been nice."

He'd actually thought that himself. "I'm sure Aunt Eileen won't object if you go ahead and bring a Helen into the family." Normally, teasing Grace about having babies to make their aunt happy would have had him grinning from the inside out, but not today. It was an effort to even carry on a conversation. The trip to Fancy's old apartment yesterday had been a bust. When the friend finally came home from work she apologized up and down but swore that Fancy had only stayed with her a few weeks before heading to Los Angeles. Something about Fancy getting a better offer but the woman had no details or data.

"Well, we're not going there," Grace turned off the road and under the arch onto the ranch drive. "I'm personally very thankful to you and Brooks for taking some of the pressure off to reproduce. Connor too. With three young'uns in the house, Aunt Eileen should be seriously busy for a good long while."

Not much scared Ethan. He thrived on adrenaline rushes. Exploring the unknown. Pushing the limits. His career choice hadn't come with any promises of security. But at this very moment, as the house he grew up in grew larger in the distance, he was scared down to his socks. What did he know about babies, children, and parenting? It was one thing to have a buddy's back, but to be responsible for the nurturing and upbringing of a tiny human being? What if he totally screwed it up? Wasn't an absentee father a major cause of dysfunctional children—and military life certainly qualified for absentee. In his case, very absentee.

The sedan came to a stop by the front porch and before Ethan could shift around, the door flew open and his aunt was at his side. "Don't you move. Your father's coming out to help."

"I don't need help, Aunt Eileen." Ethan spun about, setting his feet on the ground.

"I'll get the crutches." Grace slammed her door shut and yanked the rear door open, grabbing them from the back seat, and then hurried around to Ethan's side.

"Thanks." By the time he'd pushed to his feet, well, foot, half the family had huddled around him like a football team protecting their quarterback.

"Be careful." Aunt Eileen held her arms out in preparation to stop his fall if he lost his balance. The maternal wishful thinking almost made him smile.

"Yes, ma'am." He might be nervous and uncertain of his future but he hadn't totally lost his mind. Arguing with his aunt had never been a good idea growing up and he didn't see any reason to point out the absurdity of her efforts now.

"Give the man some space," his father said with the wave of an arm. "Glad to have you home, son."

Ethan nodded. Adam and Brooks had followed his father and aunt and now stood off to one side. Each nodded and smiled at him. Neither needed to say anything, Ethan understood, they were there for him. He hadn't needed to join the Marines to understand the significance of Semper Fi, his family had taught him the meaning of *always faithful* and never leave a man behind, from the time he could walk. Even if, in the case of the Farradays, never leaving a man behind was more akin to not leaving a brother to take the heat for whatever crazy-ass stunt one of them had pulled.

The trunk slammed shut and DJ appeared behind his brothers, Ethan's duffel bag in hand. "I hope you're hungry. Aunt Eileen has been cooking for days. There's enough food to feed your entire platoon."

Ethan hadn't had a decent appetite since waking up in the hospital. Even now the smells of roasted meat and what he was pretty sure was his favorite green bean casserole did little to entice his taste buds. "A bit."

Several pairs of eyes glanced back and forth at each other before crossing into the house.

Becky was the one to come bouncing out of the kitchen and screech to a halt a few feet in front of him.

"It's okay. I won't break." Ethan knew she couldn't have

changed that much in only a few months and yet, somehow the pipsqueak seemed all grown up. He forced a reassuring smile. "I promise."

Slowly, Becky closed the gap between them and, careful not to nudge the crutches, wrapped her arms around him. "Welcome home."

Funny how so much could change in such a short amount of time. To anyone watching, the loving welcome looked very much like any other time she'd hugged him or given him a peck on the cheek, but Ethan felt the difference. Not so much in the physicality, but somehow it was just...different. And no surprise there. She was in love with DJ now. Balancing on the crutches and unable to hug her back, Ethan simply looked over her shoulder to his older brother. DJ was a good man. All his brothers were, but still. Pinning DJ with his gaze, Ethan conveyed the same thing he would have said to any man who captured the heart of Becky Wilson—watch it.

With a blink of his eyes, and the slightest dip of his chin, DJ answered—message received. Then his gaze shifted warmly to Becky and Ethan knew those words would never need to be said again. "Okay," DJ stepped forward. "That's enough family love."

Becky giggled and slid against DJ, fitting just right under his arm. Her fingers threaded with the hand hanging over her shoulder. Oh yeah. Ethan wouldn't ever have to worry.

"I'd better get back into the kitchen," Aunt Eileen shuffled around him, and he was pretty sure he caught her swiping quickly at one eye. "I was mid whip with the mashed potatoes. And you," she waved a finger in the direction of a new furniture addition to the living room, "go sit."

His father nodded. "We figured you'd be more comfortable in a recliner than sprawled out on a sofa with a pile of pillows."

Ethan nodded. Too many vets came home to little or no support system. He was definitely damn lucky with his lot in life.

"We've been waiting for you." Wiping her hands on an apron, Meg strolled from the large kitchen into the den.

Ethan looked up from the recliner he'd just sunk into and reached for the lever to lower the footrest.

"No. Don't get up." She leaned over and squeezed his neck in a strong hug, and whispered. "It's going to be okay."

Ethan blinked and nodded.

Meg straightened and smiled. "We ran out of oven space so all the baking is getting done next door. Toni and Catherine are in charge. I don't think Catherine has a clue what she volunteered for, but Toni will bring her up to speed."

Ethan nodded again, and scanned the room. Where was Brittany? He'd expected her to be cradled in one of the women's arms and thrust at him the second he walked through the door. Was it that obvious to everyone how unprepared he was for this whole situation?

Meg's smile broadened. "Finn's got her. Ready to meet your daughter?"

How did she know he was looking for the baby? Then what she'd said registered. "Finn?" The guy was great with animals, but human babies?

Adam chuckled "Yeah. Turns out that of all of us, he's great at Uncle Mom."

Before Ethan's mind could contemplate the implications of that statement, six feet of cowboy stood at Ethan's side with a sleeping rag doll sprawled over his shoulder.

"Should you be holding her like that?" Ethan asked.

A hand on the baby's back, Finn shrugged the other shoulder. "She has a little trouble with gas every now and again. She likes the pressure from my shoulder." With surprising ease, Finn patted the sleeping baby at the same time he slid her down till her bottom rested on his forearm and her head snuggled just under his chin. "When she's happy and sleepy she likes this spot best. I think it's because she feels my heart."

Ethan knew he was gawking. Finn hadn't had any different training than any of the brothers. He hadn't been prone to playing with dolls and, like himself and DJ, Finn had been too young to help with Grace when she'd been born. "Where did you learn all this?"

Finn shrugged again. "Not much to learn. Just common sense."

Common sense? Ethan had plenty of that. Street sense too. Both had kept him alive and healthy. But...

"Ready?" Finn leaned forward, the baby slipping easily into position on Finn's proffered hands. His brother clearly meant to hand off the infant and Ethan thought for the first time in his life he might have a panic attack. Before he could utter a sound, Finn's voice rumbled with laughter.

Ethan could hear the muffled sound of his other brothers chuckling too. Bug eyed, Ethan's gaze swung to the traitorous siblings. Adam and Brooks had the decency to clear their throats and put on a straight face. Not DJ. Arms crossed, he merely smiled even wider.

"She's not going to break." Finn extended his arms closer to Ethan's chest and the little arms and legs in pink coveralls wiggled. "Better hurry, she's about to wake up."

Before he knew exactly how it happened, Ethan had about thirteen pounds of tiny human in his hands.

"Keep holding her like a sack of flour and she's not going to be happy." Finn reached over. "Turn her—"

"What?" Ethan's head snapped up toward his brother. *Turn*?

"Lord spare me new fathers." Finn huffed out a breath and shook his head. "Put your eyes back in your head. Maneuver, is that better?" Finn cradled Brittany's head in the palm of his hand and helped his brother reposition her so her bottom was in one hand and her head rested in the crook of Ethan's arm, then Finn straightened and stepped back. "Now, was that so hard?"

At that moment dark lashes lifted up and bright eyes gazed up at him.

Bracing to have the baby scream bloody murder at this clumsy oaf holding her, Ethan was instead sucked in by the way the little girl studied him. She seemed to be taking in every feature from the roots of his hair to the cleft in his chin. As her eyes zeroed in on his, her legs pulled up and kicked out. Instinctively he placed his hand over her tummy and with unexpected agility for one so small, Brittany reached out and snatched his thumb.

A sudden swell in his chest forced all the oxygen held in his lungs out in a rush. Her feet pumped one more time, her hand shook his, and the corners of her mouth lifted upward. She was smiling at him. Emotions tumbled about inside him faster than he could identify. Joy, love, pride and for the first time since hearing of her arrival—anger. Not at Brittany, but at Fancy. *In a box under a bench.* The fury at the mother of his child spiked only to be squelched by another kick, another shake and a small gurgling noise to accompany the smile. His little girl. His to love and protect. No one was ever going to put her in harms way again. Ever.

Ethan had no idea how he was going to raise this child alone and do right by her, but do right he would. He dragged his gaze away from his daughter—*his daughter*—and looked up to see his entire family circling him, staring, including Connor with a young girl on his shoulders, and Connor's new other half. He hadn't heard them come in. Every last person in the room was grinning at him like damn Cheshire Cats. And he couldn't blame them.

Shifting his attention to DJ, Ethan sucked in a deep breath. "Whatever it costs, I want the best lawyer your friend can recommend. With or without Fancy's help, I want everything finalized so I can be damn sure no one can ever take Brittany away from me."

Brittany tugged at his finger, demanding his attention. Ethan smiled back at his little girl. Heaven help anyone who tried to come between him and his daughter. "Semper Fi, baby girl." *Semper fi.*

CHAPTER FOUR

A million things ran through Allison's mind during the long drive home. Planning, organizing, categorizing, and follow-through had been her strengths most of her life. It was one of the skills that made her a good team leader working for MHI. By the time she'd finished processing what the investigator had told her yesterday afternoon about her sister's life since Francine had left home all those years ago —what they could track—Allison's head was spinning. Even a night's sleep at the roadside motel midway between San Diego and home hadn't helped clear her mind. And now, crossing the Golden Gate Bridge, after hours of thinking, she didn't understand any better how her sister could have just left her own flesh and blood with a damn near stranger—in a box.

The one thing she did feel for sure was that Brooklyn hadn't lied. According to the minimal documentation she'd received, the family had asked her for a medical history. Apparently someone was thinking ahead. That made her feel moderately better. But it was her own research that had put her more at ease. Enough to get the first decent night's sleep since learning she had a niece. With a name, she'd been able to do a quick search with her phone on the family caring for Brittany. Only able to scratch the surface, she was eager to get home, get on her desktop, talk to her lawyer, and arrange for a trip to West Texas. ASAP.

Her dashboard lit up with an incoming call and Allison hit the answer button on her steering wheel. "Did you miss me?"

Mark, her mentor, and head of her department at County Hospital, responded. "What's your ETA?"

His tone had her on alert. "About thirty minutes from home."

"And the hospital?"

"Next exit."

"Good. There's been an emergency. Car accident. An expectant mother, twenty-eight weeks. Stevens is on his way but I'd rather have you on this one."

She glanced at the clock. Whatever distress the fetus was in had to be dicey if Mark was willing to wait for her. Texas and her niece would have to wait at least another day.

● ● ● ●

"You're going to have to go before a judge." Grace passed the bowl of garlic and cheddar mashed potatoes to her right.

"That doesn't make sense." Connor grabbed a biscuit and looked to his fiancée.

It had only been a few hours since Ethan had come through the front door, and already all his siblings, and the newest additions to the family, soothed his soul like a balm.

Catherine shrugged. "I don't do family law, but I do know that much. Signing an affidavit relinquishing parental rights is only the first step. To be effective you'll have to go to court and get a judgment for termination."

"See." Grace stuck her tongue out at her brother. "We're lucky the promulgated form that woman used covered all the key things needed to be acceptable to a judge."

"And that she had it notarized," Catherine added. "I just wish she'd had it witnessed too."

Grace nodded. "Normally an irrevocable termination of parental rights like that woman signed—"

"Francine," Ethan corrected. He didn't know why, in many ways he agreed with his sister. Anyone who left her child in a damn box on the doorstep didn't deserve the respect of a given name, and yet, Fancy would always be Brittany's mother. Somehow *that woman* just didn't seem right.

Graced rolled her eyes, reminding Ethan of the petulant teen who used to occupy that spot at the dining room table. "Fran-cine,"

Grace enunciated carefully, "should also have had it signed by two witnesses, but a good judge shouldn't have any doubts that Francine's behavior is not in Brittany's best interest."

Catherine extended her arm and closed her hand around his brother Connor's. The fingers slipped into place like they'd always been two halves of a whole, but the quick tightening of her grip told Ethan even more. Grace may be convinced there was no problem with missing witness signatures, but Catherine was not of the same opinion.

"What about the rest of her family?" Sean Farraday looked to his police chief son. "The sister. Have they found her yet?"

"They never lost her. She was just unreachable until a couple of weeks ago." DJ set his knife and fork down. "I was going to wait until after dinner, but—"

"But what?" Ethan's meal churned in his stomach.

"I got a call from Brooklyn a little while ago. Yesterday one of his operatives gave the sister Ethan's name and our request for a family medical history."

"The sister didn't know Ethan's name?" Aunt Eileen spoke up for the first time since the conversation had shifted to talk of Brittany's mother.

"They're estranged," Ethan explained. Fancy had mentioned her sister a few times. She was extremely proud of her, which was why it had surprised him when Fancy had told him she hadn't seen her sister since they were teenagers.

DJ nodded. "The sister didn't even know Francine had a baby."

"And…" their father prompted.

"The sister is not at all happy Francine gave Ethan the baby."

"Yeah, well…" Sean shifted in his seat and Ethan could tell his father was measuring his words carefully. "This isn't about what makes the sister happy."

"No. No, it's not." DJ turned to Grace and then to Catherine. Both were looking at him with pinched lips. "Telling her who Ethan is seemed like the only way to get her to give up any information she might have had on Francine. After all, you were the ones to say having Francine sign a new affidavit with witnesses would go a long way to securing Ethan's rights and protecting Brittany."

Catherine blew out a sigh.

"I still don't like it," Grace set her napkin on the table and pushed her chair back. "I think I need dessert."

Ethan looked to Catherine. "Can the sister make trouble for us?"

Catherine's eyes twinkled and her lips curled up in a smile. "Totally not what you asked me, but I have to say, you men amaze me. Every last one of you are too good to be true."

"Excuse me?" Connor flashed her an exaggerated wide-eyed grin.

Shaking her head at her fiancé, Catherine turned to face Ethan. "I'm just saying, most men in your position would be working overtime to disprove paternity, or at least unburden themselves from any responsibility."

"That's not the Farraday way," Ethan said before his father could. Not that his first reaction to the news of his progeny hadn't been *no way*. "So, what is the answer?"

"Yes and no. The aunt's relationship is legally beneath yours. As Brittany's father of record on the birth certificate and as will be documented with the new DNA tests ordered while you were still in the hospital, the aunt's interests do not supersede yours."

"I sense a 'but' coming." Adam took hold of his wife Meg's hand. Every person at the table was watching Catherine intently. Only little Stacy was more interested in the baby sleeping a few feet away in the porta-crib.

"But," Grace spoke up, "her objections *could* sway the judge against approving the request for termination of rights."

"Damn," Ethan mumbled softly, and several similar murmurs sounded around the table.

"Not necessarily," Catherine said, "but moving forward sooner rather than later would be a good idea."

Ethan nodded. From the moment he'd extricated himself from the shattered helo, his first and only thought had been to get himself back in shape and back into the cockpit. Ever since laying eyes on his daughter he'd struggled to wrap his brain around being a father. Now he had to push through fast and hard to figure out how to pull off both.

CHAPTER FIVE

"She's beautiful, isn't she?" Aunt Eileen came to stand beside Ethan.

"I hope you're not expecting an argument from me?" The portable crib had been set up in the family room all week. There was only so much Ethan could do with the baby while staying off his feet. He'd become very good at watching her sleep from his designated spot in the recliner. With his one hand still in a protective bandage he'd shied away from diapers for now, but after supervising his aunt and his brother, Ethan was convinced there was nothing to it. "By the way," he waited for her to glance away from the baby and at him. "Thanks."

His aunt's gaze sparkled at him. "You know I love babies."

"I do. But thank you anyhow. It can't be easy getting up with her at night, taking care of both of us all day." Unfortunately, with his leg, it would be at least a couple more weeks before he'd be able to pace with the baby and help with middle-of-the-night feedings.

"Pretty soon you'll get the okay to walk on that thing, then you can let the rest of us sleep through the night." Aunt Eileen's stern words came through a smile.

Truth was, when he was able to walk and help out more his aunt probably wouldn't let him. Heck, according to DJ and Becky, as soon as Ethan was made aware of Brittany and made his intentions clear to get leave and do right by her, his aunt had scooped her up lock, stock, and diaper bag and brought her home to the ranch.

"She seems to be sleeping a little longer every night. I guess you were right about that contraption." More than once his father and aunt had insisted the secret was the insanely expensive English style baby carriage his aunt had ordered to replace the rusty one in the attic.

"That contraption is worth every penny, trust me. Whenever Brittany starts to stir, I stick out my arm and grip the handle, rock her a little. She falls back asleep for a few minutes. I keep doing this until she demands her midnight snack."

"Is that what Mom did with us?"

"I think so. I was doing things the hard way when Grace was born." His aunt cupped her hand across the back of the sleeping baby's head. "Adam was the one who mentioned to me that your mom kept the carriage close to the bed. It wasn't hard for me to figure out the rest from there."

Ethan nodded, not that he was convinced he would have figured anything out on his own.

"Any word from that fancy lawyer yet about that affidavit?"

"Nothing new. All we can do is wait for our turn on the court docket."

"Hmm," Aunt Eileen groused, then stepping away from him, wiped her hands on the back of her jeans. "I'm gonna change into a shirt that hasn't been spat up on. I've got to pick up some supplies in town. Grace should be back from working with Finn soon and agreed to watch the baby. Thought you might enjoy a change of scenery after being cooped up here all week."

"You got that straight." Sitting in a chair all day with nothing to do but think was a sure way to drive a man slowly crazy. Even with a beautiful new daughter to stare at.

"Soon as your sister is ready, we'll head out. If Brittany wakes up wanting her bottle, just talk to her till I come back."

Ethan nodded at his aunt's back. No sooner had she climbed the stairs than Brittany's eyes popped open. He'd noticed tended to look around and take in her surroundings before letting anyone know she was awake. According to his aunt that meant she was very smart and absorbing information. The point was mentioned and debated more than once at the dinner table. Finn, the one who had dubbed the baby Bree as an alternate to Grace's nickname of Peanut, believed it simply meant she'd been born a wise, easygoing soul. Grace leaned toward her aunt's philosophy, and that Brittany of course took after Grace in the smarts department. The only conclusion the dinner table had reached was that Grace may have turned out to be pretty smart, but as an infant she was far from easygoing, and whether or not studying her surroundings was an indication of intelligence was irrelevant because Brittany was definitely a smart baby.

Brittany's gaze shifted to his direction and when she saw his face she smiled. He loved that she recognized him already. That was his story and he was sticking to it. "Hey, precious. You have a nice nap?"

Dressed in only a pale green T-shirt and a diaper, Brittany waved her arms, kicked her legs and the tip of that little pink tongue peeked out between her gummy laugh.

"I'll take that as a yes. You think if your dad took a shot at changing that wet diaper you could not squirm so I can do this one handed?" Both her arms and legs went perfectly still and Ethan actually blinked, waiting for her to wiggle. When she didn't move a muscle, he shrugged. "Well then, I guess that's also a yes. I'm game if you are."

Ethan lifted himself from the chair and, leaning on the crutches as much as possible, placed himself strategically beside the portable crib for extra balance. Reaching for a fresh diaper, he set it and the wipes beside her. "This is going to be a piece of cake." Though he wasn't sure for whose benefit that announcement had been, his or hers.

No longer smiling, Brittany once again studied him intently. When he'd peeled open the diaper, he gave up a silent prayer of thanks that it was only wet. A couple of quick wipes and he blew out a relieved breath. It hadn't occurred to him that he'd be fearful of hurting her. He'd never considered his hands to be that large. Mostly average for a man of his size. But touching such a smooth, soft and delicate little person made him acutely aware of how big and rough his hands actually were.

Now came the fun part. His aunt usually grabbed Brittany by the ankles with one hand, lifted her bottom slightly, and then slid the clean diaper under. Gripping anything with his injured hand wasn't really an option yet, but he was a Marine, he'd figured out more complicated situations than this. Wobbling slightly in place he shook out the folded diaper and set it down. Brittany gave her feet a little kick and Ethan laughed. Only a few months old and already reprimanding her old man for taking too long. "Okay. Let's try this." Lifting her legs with his good hand he shimmied the clean diaper under her bottom part-way, then did the same with the other side. Making progress, he decided this would work and a couple more maneuvers had the diaper mostly under her bottom. "Close enough for government work," he mumbled.

Even though he didn't have the fine motor skills back to grip anything with his fingers, at least he was able to set his bad hand on the folded-over diaper to hold it in place. He peeled the protective paper off the tab, and bringing it forward, taped the bottom to the top. He repeated the step with the other side and smiled proudly at Brittany, even if the diaper looked a bit lopsided.

Arms waving and legs kicking again, Brittany seemed to be as proud of his accomplishment as he was. If only he could carry her into the kitchen and fix her bottle like normal dads. And that thought brought on still another. If only he could be home to watch her grow up like normal dads. Or would he? According to Brooks his foot was progressing better than he would have expected. For Ethan, every day wiggling his toes felt like less of a struggle, but something in his gut told him he wasn't out of the woods yet.

Setting the crutches between the chair and crib and balancing on one good leg, he used his bandaged hand more for ballast than anything and scooped Brittany up and against his chest, then swung around and half hobbled back into the recliner. With the baby snuggled on his lap and playing with the thumb of Ethan's bad hand, it struck him that he might have just found the one thing he loved more than flying for Uncle Sam.

• • • •

A cowboy, horses, and the dry western landscape looked way more romantic on the big screen or TV than it did at a Texas truck stop. The only thing Allison could make out of the horses in the parked trailers was that they were big. Really big. And as for the cowboys, she figured they were the real deal, but the few she'd seen today were rather scrawny looking in dusty jeans and the clinking sound when they walked had quickly gotten on her nerves. At first she didn't quite know what it was and then she realized at least one of the men in boots had what she assumed were spurs on. Though why they'd have on spurs to drive a trailer of horses from point A to point B she didn't have a clue.

The Farradays might be nice people, but increasing visions of her niece growing up in overalls and chewing on the stem of a corn pipe, or up to her knees in manure, had Allison more convinced than ever that coming to Texas was the right decision. Sooner rather than later. She'd had plenty of time to think about it and still didn't have a clue what she would do. According to the attorneys she'd spoken with, the father held all the cards, but she had to come up with something.

"Why would anyone put a town all the way out here?" For twenty minutes she'd been waiting for some sign of life. The first one had come as a big old antebellum mansion surrounded by building supplies and a few men and trucks appeared not far from the main road. At least that gave her hope the GPS wasn't totally wrong. Now her heart practically leapt at the cluster of buildings on the horizon. Her stomach growled loudly, reminding her that the bag of chips and cola she'd picked up at the last stop a couple of hours ago had long worn off. Since the only place to stay in town was a bed and breakfast, and they weren't expecting her this early, the building ahead with the neon café light called her name.

Pulling into the parking lot, Allison stepped out of the car and looked around. The immediate impression caught her off guard. She knew in her mind that the picture of dirt roads, wood planked sidewalks, and hitching posts was absurd in the twenty-first century, and yet the pretty brick buildings and concrete sidewalks still came as a surprise. If anything, the main street reminded her more of Mayberry than the anticipated Wild Wild West.

"Afternoon." An older gentleman in mechanic's coveralls smiled as he passed on his way into the restaurant then caught her off guard again when he stood holding the door for her.

"Oh. Thank you." Inside the place definitely felt like she'd stepped back in time. Not the shiny metallic look of chic retro restaurants imitating an era long gone, but just a cozy older place with well worn but not shabby furnishings and decor. The old man sat at a stool along the counter in front of her, but she wanted to sit someplace a bit more hidden. Already several heads had turned to look her over. As cute as the town seemed, she suspected this place wasn't on the hit parade of tourist attractions and that all the people casually staring her way were locals.

"Take a seat anywhere, honey," a woman in her mid-thirties, give or take a few years, smiled, handed Allison a menu, and waved an arm around the eatery.

Returning the smile, Allison turned right to the side of the café filled with booths and grabbed the one at the end. She had a pretty good view of most of the place and was finding it rather fascinating. Apparently Texas really was the friendly state as one of the road signs had declared. So far people were smiling at each other and chatting on their way to or from a table. The waitress who had greeted her at the door referred to everyone by name. More than once a stranger had made eye contact with her and rather than turn away, they'd smiled and nodded as though she were any one of the locals they'd known for years.

The waitress set a glass of water on the table. "Special of the day is Frank's meatloaf, but he outdid himself with the beef stew today."

"Oh," Allison had been thinking salad, but suddenly that beef stew sounded pretty good. "Hmm."

Instead of getting huffy while Allison wasted her time, the

woman bit back a knowing smile. "The salad's not bad either, but the meatloaf and the stew come with homemade buttermilk biscuits."

"Stew," Allison said in a snap. The San Francisco bay area might be a mecca of diverse culinary banquets, but the way the word *homemade* rolled off the waitress' tongue already had Allison's mouth watering.

Without the menu for camouflage to people watch, Allison pulled out her e-reader and opened to one of her favorite authors. A few pages into the book, a bowl of piping hot stew appeared in front of her followed by a small dish with two biscuits and scoops of butter. "Hope you're not on a diet. The butter is real. I recommend spreading it while the biscuit's still warm."

Allison didn't waste any time. She broke the biscuit open, felt the rush of warmth escape from the doughy center and slathered on a large chunk of butter. She'd worry about clogged arteries another day. The waitress was still at her side when Allison bit into the biscuit. "Oh. My God." Her eyes fell closed and Allison heard herself groan with delight.

"I see you'll do anything to win over new customers."

Allison's eyes snapped open at the deep voice. Heat instantly surged up her neck and settled in her cheeks. A policeman, no less. What would all the patrons looking her way think if she just slid under the table?

"Don't you go picking on my customers, DJ, just because they recognize good home-cooked food."

The policeman had the decency to look contrite and, staring Allison straight in the eye, dipped his chin and offered a polite smile. "Sorry, ma'am. No offense intended."

"That's more like it." The waitress nodded.

The way the waitress—Allison took a second to read the tag on the woman's breast pocket—Abbie teased the man there had to be more than a business relationship. On the other hand, hadn't Allison seen her tease and visit with just about everyone in the place?

"I'm waiting on my brother and my aunt. I'll take a booth so he can stretch his leg out."

"Of course." Abbie smiled at him and waved a finger at the window. "I see you're in the cruiser."

That must have had some significance because the guy's grin grew impossibly wider. "And not soon enough. A man can only take so much desk duty. Feels good to be back again."

"'Bout time those investigators wrapped things up." Her lips pressed tightly together, Abbie nodded at him before taking a step back. "I'll get you some coffee and pie while you're waiting."

"What is it today?" he asked.

"Sweet potato." She grinned and walked away.

Hanging his hat on the nearby hook, he turned to face Allison. "I really am sorry if I made you uncomfortable. Abbie and I go back a long way and it's hard to pass up a chance to tease her."

"No problem. I might have gotten carried away just a little, but they're so good. I can't decide if it's the biscuit or the butter—"

"A bit of both I suppose. Frank makes the best biscuits in the county but if all you've ever had is store bought butter, then the real stuff seals the deal."

"I guess so." Allison had heard of friendly small town attitudes, but she'd always thought the occasional smile and nod from her Marin County neighbors was the same thing. She couldn't imagine this much conversation back home from someone she'd never met before. Not knowing what else to do, she smiled one last time then stabbed at her stew and pretended to read her book.

"It's over!"

Allison looked up in time to see a beaming older woman tear across the café and practically fly into the policeman's arms. Her hands went up to either side of his face and she stared up at him with pride and joy and an overload of love. Was this the aunt he told the waitress he was waiting for? The two looked more like mother and son. The whole scene made Allison smile.

Just as Allison was about to look away, the older woman's gaze caught hers and Allison desperately wanted to crawl under the table. She hated getting caught spying. "Sorry, I didn't mean to eavesdrop."

"Nonsense," the woman waved off her apology. "I wasn't exactly trying to keep a secret." Her arm shot out at Allison. "Eileen Callahan. You passing through or staying for a visit?"

Momentarily surprised, Allison accepted the proffered hand. "I'm not sure how long I'll be here yet."

"Don't let our sleepy town fool you, we've got some charming little shops and if you like ghost towns we're on the ghost town circle."

"Ghost town?" *Seriously?*

The policeman smiled. "The only thing Texas has more of than cows and oil wells is ghost towns. Over nine hundred. Someone came up with the idea of drawing a line from abandoned town to town and turns out West Texas has a circle of abandoned property no one wants to live in."

"My niece owns the bed and breakfast in town and she has all kinds of information and maps on what to do in the area."

"Oh, I believe I have a reservation there. That is, if it's still the only accommodations in town."

"It is." Eileen rubbed her hands together. "You're going to love it."

The policeman, DJ, waved a hand up in the air and the other woman turned to flag down the man coming through the door. Tall, broad shouldered in jeans, a light blue button-down shirt, and what Allison guessed was a real Stetson, this was what she'd expected a Texas cowboy to look like. Except for the crutches. And even so he had a swagger that drew her eyes straight to the massive shiny buckle on his belt.

"How ya holding up, bro?" The policeman asked.

"Great."

Allison shouldn't have been listening, but something in the approaching man's voice had reached down inside her and latched on. She couldn't stop peeking over the top of her e-reader.

"Stopped a minute to say hi to Becky." The man on crutches had turned his back to her and was hanging his hat on a pole hook at the edge of the booth. She wasn't sure but she thought she saw the policeman bristle slightly. "Wanted to thank her for helping you. Means a lot to me."

The officer's shoulders clearly relaxed. "I'm sure she appreciated it."

The cowboy turned in her direction as he bent to slide into the booth. A slight grimace tensed around his mouth.

"Right." The policeman shook his head. "I can see how great you're feeling. You're supposed to stay off that leg for a reason."

"I'm fine." Scooting back, the cowboy smiled at his brother. He had a nice profile to match the voice. "If I don't move around at least a little I'll be a ninety pound weakling when I can finally chuck these crutches."

Somehow she doubted he'd ever be a weakling. She continued to dig into the stew and focused on her book. In the adjacent booth, the banter continued between the two men and their aunt. There were chuckles and jokes. Apparently what the aunt had been so excited about was that a police incident had been investigated and the man Allison now realized was the police chief had been cleared of any wrongdoing and was back in charge of the town. She didn't know why but for some reason that made her happy. She liked these people. The words on the electronic page faded as she found herself instead daydreaming about how different things might have been if her parents hadn't died young, if her own aunt had had a rapport with her and Francine the way this woman seemed to have with her nephews. The three formed the perfect picture. Then again, there was no such thing as the perfect family. Everyone had skeletons or black sheep.

Taking in the last bite of stew on her plate, she set the ebook down and looked up in search of the waitress. At that moment the man with the delicious voice and shiny buckle turned to his aunt and his beautiful green eyes locked with hers. His brows curled into a question seconds before his eyes opened wide with surprise. Holy moly. What the hell was the guy from the park in San Diego doing in this little Texas town?

CHAPTER SIX

than had to blink. Twice. And then again. Surely his eyes were playing tricks on him. No way the beautiful brunette in the booth behind them was the same woman from the park in San Diego. It just wasn't possible.

"What's wrong?" His aunt stretched her arm across the table and rested her hand on his.

When he spotted the same surprise he felt reflected back in the woman's eyes, he knew. It had to be her.

"Ethan?" Aunt Eileen tried again.

The concern in his aunt's voice pulled him back to her question. "Nothing, just a little surprised." He'd heard of small worlds but this was just a bit on the ridiculous side. Excitement at getting another chance to chat with her warred with a wariness from years on the battlefield. Shame on anyone who bought into something too good to be true. They usually found themselves owners of beachfront property in the desert.

"Hi." Her voice came out a little shaky.

He couldn't blame her. He was feeling rather shaken-up himself. A smile might be appropriate. Camouflage. Never let them see you sweat. "Hello."

His aunt turned her head to look at the young lady and back at him.

"Glad to see you've at least got the leg elevated," the brunette said, her smile a little stronger.

"Yeah. It's coming along."

"Good. Good."

His aunt looked back and forth again and this time DJ was the one with a frown on his face. "I gather you two know each other?" DJ asked.

"Not exactly." The woman tilted her head as though studying him. Only a hint of a smile now teased her lips, but the concern in her gaze no doubt kept it at bay.

"We met briefly in California," he explained.

All the color drained from his aunt's face, her head snapped around to look at the woman again and then twisted back just as quickly to stare questioningly at Ethan. It took him a few seconds to read the panic in her eyes. He shook his head. No, this wasn't the mother of his child. Fancy was a plastic, tired, blue-eyed natural blonde. The gal across looked way younger than the years she'd have to be for a doctor and her gray eyes played well against her dark hair.

His aunt blew out a heavy breath and Ethan twisted his hand from under hers to give a reassuring squeeze.

"You must live around here?" The brunette's eyes narrowed in thought. She was struggling hard to make sense of the coincidence.

"Technically I live in California, but this is home."

"Oh. I see." The hesitation in her voice said exactly the opposite. "Where's your dog?"

"My dog?"

His aunt snapped her head around again and mumbled *dog*.

"The one that stole my lunch."

Ethan shook his head. "I don't have a dog. I thought he was yours."

"Nope." The woman shook her head.

His aunt turned her head back and forth, keeping up with the conversation like a proverbial tennis match, her eyes growing with interest. "What kind of dog?"

They both looked to his aunt, but she was the first to speak. "Shaggy."

"Shaggy?" The corner of his aunt's lips tilted up in a slight smile.

Ethan ignored his aunt. "He didn't look like a stray. I guess he belonged to someone else at the park."

"Stray?" his aunt repeated, her grin growing.

DJ coughed and swallowed a smile of his own. What the heck was up with these two?

At his muffled cough, the lady turned to his brother, who was leaning against the window. Her gaze drifted over his shoulder and she raised her hand to point. "Like that one."

All heads in Ethan's booth whipped around to the large dog sitting on the curb, staring up at the café window. DJ laughed outright.

"He's back." His aunt rubbed her hands together with vigor and turned to the woman. "Isn't this nice. I didn't catch your name."

"Allison."

"And what did you say brought you to Tuckers Bluff?"

"Business. Personal business." Her gaze met Ethan's and he had a terrible feeling in the pit of his stomach that he wasn't going to like whatever that business was.

"Well," his aunt straightened in her seat, "as soon as you get settled in, we'll have to have Adam, my nephew, bring you to the ranch. Like I said before, his wife runs the bed and breakfast you're staying at. I'd be pleased to show you some true Texas hospitality."

"Aunt Eileen," DJ's words were said softly, but through his teeth.

Ethan was definitely missing something.

"It's been a long flight and drive. I just need to rest up a bit and then tend to my business. But I appreciate the offer, Mrs. Callahan."

"Mrs. Callahan was my mother. Most folks call me Aunt Eileen." She turned to DJ. "Go ahead and tell her she's perfectly safe with us."

"I'm not so sure about that," DJ mumbled.

"Oh," Allison's hand flew to her chest and her eyes rounded. "I didn't mean to imply—"

"Of course not." Aunt Eileen waved off her concerns. "No

offense taken, but you can't pass through town without at least trying my glazed Texas pecan pie. I insist." Aunt Eileen turned to Ethan. "Why don't you extend a proper invitation to the lady, maybe it will sound better from a nice *single* gentleman."

Oh hell, Ethan sighed.

"And where are my manners. This is my other nephew, Ethan—"

That startled look returned to Allison's eyes.

"—Farraday," his aunt finished.

"Farraday?" Allison mumbled, her gaze darting from one man to the other.

"Are you all right?" DJ waved for the waitress.

Ethan almost sprang out of his seat. Like his aunt earlier, all the color had drained from the brunette's lovely face and he was a little worried she was going to keel over.

"Ready for dessert?" Abbie came up beside the table.

"I think the lady could use some more water," Ethan said.

"No." Allison shook her head. "No. I, uh, I need to get going. How far is the bed and breakfast?"

Abbie pointed a thumb over her shoulder. "Just up the road a piece."

"Good." Allison nodded. "Where do I pay the check?"

"We don't stand on ceremony around here. Usually folks pay at the register but I can take it for you."

"No. No. That's fine." She scooped up her purse and slid out of the booth. "I'll pay at the register. Turning back, she looked at the three of them, some of the color returning to her cheeks. "I will be seeing you again. Soon."

Aunt Eileen forced a smile. "I'll hold you to that."

"Yes. Goodnight."

The gal ran off like she'd seen the grim reaper himself, and Ethan figured now was as good a time as any to test his theory. "I'll be back in just a minute."

"Where are you going?" his aunt asked.

"To talk to her."

Aunt Eileen eased back in her seat. "Good idea. Go talk to her."

"Aunt Eileen," DJ uttered an exasperated sigh. Ethan would have to figure out what was going on with his brother and aunt later. Right now he had to hobble his way after the woman before she got away. He didn't know who Allison was, but he hoped to hell it had nothing to do with Brittany. Except every fiber in his body told him exactly that.

• • • •

Allison shoved the café door open, hurried to her rental car, and, safely inside, sucked in a deep breath. Ethan Farraday. The entire reason she'd flown to Texas and driven to Tuckers Bluff was to see her niece and talk face to face with Ethan Farraday. So what did she do at the first mention of his name? Run like a scared rabbit. And she was no timid bunny. She'd faced roaches the size of rats in a jungle with snakes bigger than a city sewer line while performing twenty-first century medicine in a prehistoric setting. But just the mention of his name and here she sat in a parked car.

What she needed was to get the heck out of here and regroup. She hadn't expected to run into her niece's father in the local café. Which in hindsight was probably a stupid assumption in a town this size. Nor did she expect to like them all so much. *Damn it.*

Rummaging through her purse, she found the key and placed it in the ignition. A rap on the window shoved her already unsettled nerves into overdrive. Balancing on his crutches, Ethan Farraday stood by her car door. *So much for regrouping.*

He didn't say or do anything, he merely waited for her to open her window. As soon as the glass had lowered enough, he leaned slightly forward. "Who are you?"

Resigning herself to the situation, she blew out a heavy breath. "Allison Monroe." Ethan said nothing, he simply waited for her. "My full name is Beatrice Allison Monroe."

"The sister." He shook his head, tenseness in his shoulders

told her he'd known all along what she was going to say. "We need to talk."

A nod didn't seem like enough, but her mouth wouldn't cooperate to form words.

"Not here," he added.

"Where?" she managed to ask softly.

"You asked for the B&B. Is that where you're staying?"

Allison nodded.

"I'll go get my aunt and meet you there."

"And the baby?"

His jaw tightened. "She's at the ranch."

She hadn't realized how badly she wanted to see her niece until the disappointment slammed into her at his answer. "All right. Give me a little time to settle in first."

He nodded again.

"Now if you'll excuse me." Her fingers shook slightly as she reached for the key and she hoped Ethan didn't notice.

Dipping his chin once in affirmation, he hobbled in reverse away from the door.

When she was sure he was safely away from the car, she backed out of the parking lot. In the rearview mirror she spotted that dog sitting at the edge of the lot staring in her direction. She shook her head and mumbled, "Wonder if you have any relatives in Southern California?"

CHAPTER SEVEN

Leaning heavily on one foot and rotating the other ankle, Abbie flipped the switch to brew a fresh pot of coffee and grabbed the last hot carafe. Her feet were protesting—strongly. Time for a new pair of shoes. She spent good money on the best work shoes possible, but working six and half days a week, the extra arch support had a shorter than promised life expectancy.

"Have you ever considered a day off?" Frank the cook slid a fresh pie into the display. "A full day."

"Nope." The only thing she'd gain from a long day off was 24 hours to think and remember. Work was her friend.

Shaking his head, Frank closed the glass doors. "Even Marines get some R&R."

Wasn't he one to talk. Frank worked more hours than she did. With the still warm carafe of coffee in her hand, she spun around to make the rounds again and spotted Ethan on the phone by the door. From the look on his face, she could tell the table would probably need a stiff drink but coffee would have to do.

"You seriously have to let go of the dog thing, Aunt Eileen." DJ shook his head at his aunt. "It's not like this dog is trotting across the country to pick out wives for your nephews."

"See," Eileen waved a finger at him, "you thought of it too."

Abbie bit back a chuckle. She had no idea what the heck these two were disagreeing about but if she had to place bets, she'd go with the Farraday matriarch. "More coffee?"

Aunt Eileen shook her head while DJ looked at his wrist. "Maybe one more."

"Are you giving your aunt a hard time?" she asked.

"He's just being a man," Eileen answered. "And speaking of

men, we may be a small town but we've still got some good single men."

Abbie felt a grin pull at her cheeks. From anyone else she would have taken offense. But somehow, when the ladies afternoon social club took to matchmaking, she was glad she'd never quite gotten in their crosshairs. "What can I tell you Ms. Eileen, I'm just too hot to handle."

The older woman burst out laughing. "I bet you are."

DJ winked at her and Abbie thought for the millionth time how glad she was that he'd found the perfect woman. The good guys deserved great women, and Becky was turning out to be stellar. Abbie, on the other hand, was happily married to her café. Life was just easier that way.

• • • •

Ethan paused outside the café door, pulled out his phone, and called his sister-in-law.

"Ethan!" Meg answered.

"Hey. Listen. We've got a situation."

"What's wrong?" The enthusiasm in her voice slipped away.

"You've got a guest about to check in. An Allison Monroe."

"Yes."

"She's Francine's sister."

"What?" Meg's voice rose an octave. "Isn't Francine's last name Langdon?"

"Yeah, that's her married name." He should have seen this coming.

"Wait. Married?"

He could picture the frown on Meg's face. "She's divorced." At least that was the story she'd told him and he hadn't looked that closely on the report Brooklyn had sent. "I think."

"You think?" Meg's tone took on a sharpness he hadn't heard before. "That's pretty damn important."

"And not the point at the moment."

"You want me to send her packing? I can see a double booking error creeping up."

"No—"

"If you're worried about me losing business, don't."

"Thanks, but in this case I'd rather go with keep your friends close and your enemies closer. Don't do anything differently than you normally would. But watch what you say."

"No mentioning insanity or the pesky sixth toe that runs in the family," she deadpanned. "Got it."

"Ha ha," he quipped, but he did love that Meg could say the right thing to make him bring it down a notch. "And thanks. I'll call Adam. Warn him."

"Is she that close?" Her tone grew serious again.

"Should be pulling up any second."

"Okay. Go circle the wagons and I'll see what I can find out on my end."

"You're the best."

"And I remind your brother of that every night." The humor in her voice was back.

"I bet you do." Ethan didn't like what it meant having Fancy's sister show up, but he loved that his sister-in-law had his back. And she certainly understood what it meant to be a Farraday. Circling the wagons indeed.

Yanking the door open he swung inside. Getting around on crutches was a bloody nuisance. Right about now when he wanted to move fast they upgraded to a damn nightmare. Making his way forward he moved as quickly as he could and slid into his side of the booth with more agility than he had previously.

"What's up?" DJ asked immediately.

Ethan didn't doubt that his concern showed on his face. "That was Francine's sister."

"What?" DJ and his aunt echoed.

"She'll be waiting for us at Meg's."

DJ leaned forward. "When?"

"I told her she could have a few minutes to settle in."

His aunt looked out the window and back at him. "We should call Catherine."

DJ nodded and Ethan realized his mistake. The Marine in him had no fear of charging in. But this was a different kind of battle. And Meg wasn't the only new Farraday woman who had his back. He just hoped to hell circling the wagons would be enough.

• • • •

The older lady, Aunt Eileen, had been right. The main drag led to a pretty town square and then a few more blocks to the address of the bed and breakfast. Colorfully painted, the old Victorian was as charming and pristine on the outside as the website had depicted. Glancing up the street at the considerably smaller homes, Allison suspected, once upon a time, the entire block had been its backyard.

From an early age Allison had learned the art of packing light. Leaving most of her treasured belongings to move in with her aunt Millicent had been the beginning. Off to college, then med school, and then settling into an already furnished home, she'd never needed much. The single carryon she pulled from the trunk along with her medical bag was evidence enough.

"Welcome," a tall redhead called from the front porch. "Need some help with your bags?"

"No, thanks." She slammed the hatchback door shut. "This is it." Dragging the roller bag behind her, Allison followed the pavestone path to the house. She'd expected a matronly older woman with gray hair and sensible shoes. This lady not only did not qualify for anything close to matronly, she looked like she'd stepped out of the designer section of Neiman's.

The smiling woman held the screen door open. "My name's Meg. I'll show you to your room and then you can come on down for some tea and homemade crumb cake."

"You bake?" Allison followed her up the mahogany stairs.

Meg laughed. "Not even close. But I can boil water in an

emergency."

Allison was glad to laugh back. Her stomach had been tangled in nervous tension for weeks. The knots had only tightened like wet rope upon landing on Texas soil. She was still on edge, but better. Her entire world was about to turn completely upside down if she accomplished what she'd planned. "I can relate." Fending for herself in the kitchen wasn't hard, but she'd never be one of those people who enjoyed mincing fresh herbs and creating mouthwatering meals. She'd survived med school on canned pasta and frozen dinners. Fabulous training for living in the jungle and eating things of unknown origins.

"You won't have to worry though." Meg looked over her shoulder, still smiling. "I'm not allowed to do baked goods."

"I wasn't even slightly concerned." Another knot loosened in her stomach. She liked her hostess. "Put burnt toast in front of me and I'll think it's wonderful."

Meg turned the corner at the top of the stairs. "Not fussy?"

"Blackened gluten seems a step up from some of the things I've had to eat lately."

"Oh really?" Meg pushed open a door and stepped aside. "I sense an interesting story there."

"Not really." She scanned the room quickly and almost sighed. For the first time since leaving her little cottage, she felt completely at ease. "Oh, wow."

"Nice, isn't it?" Pride shone in Meg's eyes.

"I'll say." Pale yellow walls, not quite cream, not quite sunshine, created a bright contrast to the dark wooden floors. Setting her bag down on the open luggage rack, Allison spun about. Her gaze fell on a six drawer pine dresser. Up close she ran her hand across the top and examined the iron pull. "This is an original piece. Edwardian, right?"

The redhead beamed and nodded. "England, circa 1910."

"Really nice." She looked around the room, her aunt would be impressed. "Are all these pieces original?"

Red hair slid across Meg's shoulder as her head bobbed again.

"Most of them. Yes. Some Victorian, some Edwardian. Except the bed. That's totally twenty-first century memory foam."

"Sounds heavenly." Allison patted the country quilt.

Meg led the way to the private bath. "The house runs on a tankless system so hot water is never a problem, even when we're full up."

"You had me with the bed, but with endless hot water I may never leave." The bathroom boasted white tiles from top to bottom. One side showcased a massive claw foot soaker tub and a separate walk in shower. "I bet I could sleep quite comfortably in that tub."

Meg laughed. "Where exactly have you been sleeping that a porcelain tub looks so appealing?"

Allison looked at her pristinely dressed hostess and wondered how much information would be too much. "The Amazon."

Blue eyes widened and blinked. "I gather you're not talking about the online store."

Chuckling, Allison shook her head. She really did like this lady. "Nope. The real thing."

"If you don't mind my asking, what in heaven's name were you doing there?"

"I expected a little of this and a little of that but I seemed to spend a great deal of time delivering babies and doing C-sections."

"You're a doctor?" Meg paled and her momentarily slack jawed mouth snapped shut.

Allison laughed. "Don't look so surprised. Women's lib was forty years ago."

"No. I'm sorry, it's not that, it's just—"

"Meg?" A deep voice called from downstairs. Allison had only heard it a few times, but the way the hairs on her arms stood upright, she knew who the voice belonged to.

"Don't come up. I'll be right down." Meg turned halfway around to face Allison. "As soon as you're settled in, come down for the crumb cake and tea I promised. Unless you prefer coffee, I can do that too."

A familiar discomfort settled in her stomach. No one could

get through what she had and do what she did without nerves of steel. But here and now, in this situation, with this man who the only thing she knew about was that he was her niece's father, Allison felt as skittish as a Victorian virgin bride. *Oh Fancy, what have you done?*

CHAPTER EIGHT

Halfway to the kitchen, Ethan turned to the living room and parked himself on the large leather sofa. It afforded him the ability to elevate his leg for at least a short while. He needed to be more diligent. If he wanted to get back in the cockpit he needed to get well. Fast.

Meg hopped off the last step and came to a stop in the parlor beside him. "Hi."

"I see she didn't change her mind and head back to where she came from." He pointed out the window to the car in the driveway.

"'Fraid not." Meg leaned on the sofa arm. "About that—"

"By *that* you mean *her*?"

Meg nodded. "With the exception of scumbag ex-fiancés I tend to have really good instincts."

"Okay." He certainly couldn't argue with her since she'd married his brother and her best friend married another brother.

"I know I haven't spent more than a few minutes with Allison."

A second ago *she* was *that*, now she's Allison.

"But, well," Meg shrugged, "she seems nice."

"And your point?"

"I don't know." Meg hefted her shoulder again. "I guess I was expecting something else."

Ethan couldn't argue with her there. From the few words Fancy had shared about her sister, he'd been prepared for a more grounded member of the family, but at least a little bit more like Fancy.

"I think," Meg continued, "under different circumstances, we could be friends."

"Hmm," he grunted. Mixed emotions still tumbled about

inside his head and heart. Fancy was, after all, Brittany's mother. But she'd abandoned her. And as Fancy's sister, Allison was family. And from what little he'd heard from Fancy, her dysfunctional relatives were not the kind of family he wanted Brittany influenced by. He might not be ready for father of the year, but he was pretty confident with the help of his family he'd be able to bring up a fairly well adjusted little girl. Maybe. Which brought him back to Fancy's family and concerns that input from the dysfunctional Monroes might shoot what little shot he had at getting things right straight down the tubes. "Friends," he mumbled. No. Definitely not on the agenda.

"It was just... I don't know." Meg frowned at him and then looked around. "Where's Aunt Eileen?"

"She took the truck back to the ranch."

"Why'd she do that?"

"Catherine suggested it would not be in our best interest to overwhelm Allison with our family. Yet."

"Okay." Meg seemed to take a moment to kick that idea around. "How did you get here?"

"DJ dropped me off."

"Is he taking you home or are you planning to keep your enemy even closer still and spend the night here?" A slight smile teased at the corner of her mouth, only this time he didn't find any humor in the innuendo.

That sort of behavior was what had gotten him into this mess. Not that he considered Brittany a mess, just that being a single dad hadn't been on his radar. Truthfully, being a husband and father were nowhere in his plan for putting in his twenty. Men in his kind of work made lousy husbands. "I'll hitch a ride home with Catherine."

"Catherine?" Meg's face scrunched tight in confusion. "I didn't know she was in town today."

"She's on her way. I'm supposed to not talk legal until my lawyer gets here."

"Catherine's your lawyer now?" Meg's surprise showed she

was having a hard time keeping up.

He shrugged. "She will be tonight."

"Well," Meg slapped her hands on her thighs and pushed to her feet, "I'd better put on the water for tea and hope you guys drink and chew really slow, or avoiding talking about the baby elephant in the room for over an hour until Catherine arrives will be tough." She leaned over and squeezed his shoulder. "It's going to be fine. I know it is."

Ethan hoped to high heaven his sister-in-law was right. Normally he could trust his gut, but on everything concerning Brittany and Fancy he felt like a compass without a magnet. No clue where he was going or what to do next.

"Hello again." Allison appeared in the open archway, her gaze scanning the room.

"Meg's gone to get the tea." Habit had him pushing to his feet despite the discomfort.

"Please don't." Allison waved him down. The way she hovered nearby as he took his seat again, anyone walking by would think they *were* friends.

When he settled onto the sofa, she walked to a nearby chair and instead of taking a seat, surprised him by turning back around. "You really should have that leg elevated above your heart."

"I know. It's just not convenient to lay back at the moment."

"No." She approached him with a frilly cushion in her hand. "I suppose not." Before he could process her intentions, her hand grasped his heel, lifted his leg, and slid the pillow beneath just below his knee. "Your knees should be slightly bent. Yours were locked. That puts a great deal of unnecessary stress on the joints."

"Thank you." He knew that, he just forgot to pay attention.

She eased into the smaller library chair in front of him. "You're welcome." Her gaze went over his leg and then lifted to meet his. "What did you do?"

"The easy answer is I broke it."

Apparently she had a sense of humor because a twinkle appeared in her eyes. "And how did you *break* it?"

There wasn't an easy answer to that one. "Hard landing."

Her head tilted in thought. "On what?"

"The mountainside."

This time her eyes flew open wide. "You crashed."

Obviously she knew more about him and his career than he did about hers. "Controlled hard landing."

"Does that make you feel better?"

"Excuse me?"

She shrugged. "Not using the word crash."

No pilot liked the word crash. People rarely survive crashes. He and the men in his charge had lived to tell about the *hard landing*. "I didn't realize you were a psychiatrist."

"I'm not." Her lips curved into a smile. "Just checking."

Her easy tone almost had him smiling too. He was going to have to be careful around her. Maybe his defenses were down because of the injury, or the shift in his life because of Brittany, or maybe it was just a way with this woman. Whatever, he needed to stay sharp. "You are a doctor, though?"

Dark hair brushed the sides of her cheek as her head bobbed. "Yes. I'm a surgeon."

Ethan wasn't sure why that surprised him. No matter what her specialty, it took smarts, stamina and determination to become any kind of doctor, and yet somewhere he'd felt that surgeons, good ones, required an additional gift, or talent maybe. Like a piano player with long fingers. Instantly his gaze dropped to her hands. Much like he would expect from a concert pianist. Long, slender, trimmed nails, no polish, only signs of a few healing cuts jumped at him as out of place. "Had a disagreement with a scalpel lately?"

Her fingers lifted and she glanced down at her hands before letting them fall back onto her lap. "A thorny bush."

"Like to garden?"

"Hardly. I ran after a frightened child and stumbled into an aggressive shrub. Pretty flowers. Nasty thorns."

"Here we go." Meg came into the room carrying a large silver tray and set it on the table between him and Allison and set a delicate looking cup and saucer in front of her before facing him. "This," she picked up a large white mug with the A&M logo, "is for you. It's coffee."

Pleased his sister-in-law hadn't tried to make him juggle one of those prissy tea cups, he smiled, reached for the sugar and spotted the cake balls. "Oh, man. Are those—"

"Yep," Meg smiled. "Toni dropped them off about an hour ago. I'm expecting more company and they're always a big hit at tea time."

He snatched one up covered in dark chocolate and waved it at Allison. "You're gonna love these."

Her gaze slid from him to the dessert dish of crumb cake and cake balls and back. "Recommend one in particular?"

About to pop one in his mouth, he paused, cake frozen at his lips, and shook his head. "Nope. They're all great."

She smiled hesitantly, nodded, and reached for the one with an orange tint to it.

Keeping an eye on her, his cheeks tugged at the corners of his lips as her eyes nearly rolled back in her head before she let out the tiniest bit of a moan. The cake he'd just swallowed caught in his throat and he literally shook his head to rattle the image free from his memory of her groaning with delight.

"Oh my. These are good." She smacked her lips, savoring the taste. "I can't quite—"

"Those are the mimosas." Meg grabbed one with white icing. "Champagne cake balls with Grand Marnier icing. You may want to take it easy."

"Oh," she took another bite. "Do I really have to?"

She and Meg both chuckled and Ethan saw what Meg meant. Another place and time and they probably would have been friends. What scared him more though, was another place and time and he too would have liked to be friends. Good friends.

● ● ● ●

Taking the third, and she swore last, cake ball, Allison savored every morsel. "These are insanely delicious. I mean, I've had cake balls before, but wow."

"I know. I keep telling Toni she needs to open up a professional bakery and ship these puppies out."

"Really," Allison agreed, resisting the urge to try just one more. "I can see them in every mall across America right next to the cookie and pretzel shops."

"The Texas Alcohol Beverage Commission may have something to say about that."

Allison looked to Meg. "Surely all the liquor has to be baked out of it."

"That's how it's supposed to work. Usually."

Somewhere in that last word, Allison felt sure there was a story. "Well." She took a fortifying sip of tea and set the cup down. She'd come here for a reason and she might as well start now, but where? "No sense in beating around the bush anymore. I'd like to see my niece."

Lips tightened, all Ethan did was nod.

She waited another beat or two and when she realized he wasn't going to say anything, she pushed on. "How far is the ranch from here?"

His expression was unreadable. She had a feeling she was looking at Ethan the military man. "About an hour's drive."

No surprise there. Things were awfully spread out in this part of the country. She'd figured that out pretty quickly on the drive from the airport. "Your aunt invited me to dinner."

"She didn't know who you were at the time."

Her spine stiffened. A familiar ache took root in the pit of her stomach. "Are you saying I'm not welcome...on the ranch?"

"No. I'm just not sure dinner is the answer. Especially not tonight if that's what you were thinking."

"Time is a precious commodity. I've already missed the first months of my niece's life. I've driven nearly an hour to meet a colleague in the city for dinner, driving an hour to see Francine's baby doesn't seem out of line."

"Not if that's all you want." Ethan's hard stare sent chills down her arms.

No, that wasn't all she wanted, but she wasn't ready to admit to anything more. Yet.

The roar of an engine filled the room and then cut off. The way Ethan's gaze darted to the window, Allison suspected he was expecting someone. Or maybe he was just curious. The hard steely gaze softened as another redhead hurried into the room.

Tall and slender like Meg, Allison wondered if they were perhaps siblings. One thing for sure, the lady was sharp. She took in the people in the room and assessed the situation in the blink of an eye. Her movements, graceful and measured, reminded Allison of her Aunt Millicent. Except the friendly expression meant to put everyone in the room at ease had an air of sincerity much different from her aunt's merely polite sensibilities.

A small tray in hand, Meg entered the room. "Good, you're here." She set the cup and saucer on the end table beside Ethan which would have the new arrival sitting between Allison and the stern Marine. The two women hugged and separated, and though a gentle affection was obvious, Allison ruled out sisters.

"Thanks, I could use a cup." Taking the predicted seat, the woman turned to Allison and extended her hand. "I'm Catherine."

"Nice to meet you." *Maybe*. "Allison."

"Yes," Catherine nodded.

A quick glance in Ethan's direction and she thought she spotted relief in his eyes. Appreciation perhaps, before the curtain of indifference descended again. Allison looked from Ethan to Catherine and back. "Would that be Farraday?"

Catherine's smile widened. "Not yet."

Giving a slight nod, Ethan shot the woman a gentle smile.

Nothing Allison had read mentioned anything about Ethan being in a relationship.

"I'm engaged to Ethan's brother Connor," the woman added.

"I see."

"And I'm an attorney. Though I am not Mr. Farraday's attorney of record, I am here, as a family member, to assist in ensuring his best interest—"

"And Brittany's," he interrupted.

"And Brittany's, remains at the forefront of all discussion."

Allison nodded. She hadn't quite expected such a united front. Nor had she expected Ethan's first thought to be for Brittany. He was after all a man, and a risk taker at that. Maybe she had underestimated her opponent.

"So, Miss Monroe," Catherine took a short sip and set the cup on the table, "what are your intentions?"

CHAPTER NINE

Palm flat, Finn held a treat for Brandy and scratched behind the mare's ear with his other hand. "It's a little bit crazy around here," he told the horse. "Who knew a few pounds of giggles and burps could have us all wrapped around her little finger."

The horse lifted and dipped her head and gave a low snort.

"Yeah, well, you may be the smartest one here." He ran his hand down Brandy's neck and patted her shoulder.

The horse nuzzled his empty hand and then nudged his pocket where he had the other carrot treat.

"Yep, definitely the smartest one. Here you go. Last treat and then I have to go wash up."

"Sean? Finn?" Aunt Eileen's voice carried through the horse barn.

"In here," his father answered from the tack room. "What's up?"

Finn closed the stall gate behind him and met his aunt and dad near the barn entrance.

"You'll never guess who's in town." Eileen looked from man to man.

Wiping his hands on a rag, Sean's eyes crinkled with laugh lines as he smiled at his sister-in-law. "Why don't you save us the trouble and tell us what's on your mind?"

"That woman's sister."

Finn glanced at his dad, their eyes met, and he knew they had both probably guessed right.

"And that's not all." Her expression softened. "You know who else showed up in town watching us all through the café window as though we were puppies for sale in a store window?"

The Farraday patriarch's gaze narrowed. "Don't tell me the mother's back?"

"No. The dog."

Sean Farraday's head leaned back and confusion took over his face before understanding dawned. "Oh, for Lord's sake, Eileen."

"Gray's back?" Finn smiled.

His father and aunt both snapped around to look at him.

"What? The name suits him. Or her. It was that or Terminator."

"Finn!" His aunt's jaw dropped in near horror. "That's not funny."

She was probably right. But so far that animal had saved his sister-in-law Toni from the malicious intents of her crazed then-husband, and reinforced his apparent protective nature when he'd stood his ground between Finn's soon-to-be niece Stacy and his brother Connor. "Don't look at me, Terminator was DJ's idea."

Aunt Eileen shook her head and rolled her eyes skyward much the way she'd done with him and his brothers growing up when they'd done something she considered to be absurdly ridiculous or incredibly stupid. Not that she'd ever came right out and called any of them stupid, but whenever she'd stomp off mumbling "men" they pretty much knew at that moment the two words were synonymous.

"Forget the dog," his father said, "what about the sister? Are you sure it's her?"

His aunt nodded. "She just chatted with DJ and me at the café but she told Ethan who she is. He and Catherine are talking with her right this very minute."

"Damn." Sean raked his fingers through his hair. "We'd better wash up and get to town."

"No." Eileen shook her head. "Catherine is on it and says we shouldn't all descend on the sister at once. We're to stay put until Catherine assesses the situation."

Sean paused then gave a single nod. The instincts of every member of the Farraday family was to have the back of whoever who is trouble. That included anyone who mattered to the Farradays by blood, marriage, or friendship. But if Catherine Soon-to-be Farraday said sit tight, then he would do just that.

"She's staying at the bed and breakfast."

"For how long?" Finn asked.

"Don't know. But I've been thinking on the drive back to the ranch."

"Uh-oh," Finn teased and his aunt shot him another impatient glare. He might be a legal adult, but he wasn't stupid. He bit back his mirth and let her speak.

"I think we should invite her to stay here instead."

Finn's eyes bugged open wide and his father blurted out, "Are you mad, woman?"

"Dad has a point. Acorn doesn't fall far from the tree and all that." Not that Finn believed people were destined to be good or evil by their DNA, but what little he knew from what his brother had and hadn't said, was enough to doubt the stability of this sister. Doctor or not.

"I don't think this is the case," his aunt said.

"Why? Because you saw a dog?" his dad asked pointedly.

"No, smart aleck. Because we talked at the café. She's nice. DJ said she's bashful too. And when I called Meg to see how the meeting was going she agreed. She likes her."

Sean Farraday threw his arms up in the air. "Well then by all means let's invite her into the family." He shook his head and rubbed the back of his neck. "Okay, sorry. I'll admit, if she's Brittany's kin we're going to have to learn to deal with it."

"That's right." Aunt Eileen nodded.

"But that doesn't mean we go running into a burning house with our eyes closed. Let's wait and hear what Catherine says and then find out what Ethan thinks. Brittany is his daughter."

Finn watched his aunt's face carefully. He could see the wheels turning inside that creative mind. Finally, lips pressed, she nodded. "Agreed."

"Good," Sean said, satisfied he'd made his point, but Finn

thought that battle had been too easily won. He'd be willing to bet his horse that by morning they'd have a new houseguest.

• • • •

The expression "waiting with baited breath" had never been so real to Ethan. He felt like the participant in a cruel game show and Allison's answer would be delayed until after the next commercial break.

"My intentions are, no doubt, the same as yours," she answered Catherine but studied Ethan. "What's best for my niece."

Catherine shot a sideways glance at Ethan before proceeding. "It is my understanding you have been informed that your sister relinquished her parental rights."

Allison hesitated but nodded. If he'd known her a little better he'd venture the slow swallow that preceded the nod showed how hard it was for her to accept that.

"And that Mr. Farraday is named as the father on the birth certificate?"

Allison nodded again. This time without delay or hesitation. Stranger or not, she was having as hard a time as he was understanding how Fancy could walk away from her own child.

"If you're concerned about Mr. Farraday's financial stability—"

"No. I don't have to be a detective to know the strength of the Farraday name, and most likely bank account."

"Then I don't see where you could have any concerns for—"

Staring Ethan in the eye, Allison eased forward on her seat. "Is this a career ending injury? Because last time I looked a broken ankle was not enough for the Marine Corps to send a man packing permanently."

Was that why she'd asked exactly what he'd done to his ankle? "If all goes as expected, no."

"That's what I thought." Her gaze traveled from his foot back to his eyes. "And let's say for argument's sake that you want to separate from the Marines; how long before you'll be eligible to do so?"

This gal might be a civilian doctor, but she understood enough about how leaving the Marine Corps worked. "One year."

With a curt bob of her head, she shoved herself back in the seat. "If I understand correctly, your unit is deployed to the Middle East. Even in the strongest marriages, deployments are tough. Brittany has already lost her mother, how long will she have you before you have to rejoin your unit? Will she even know who you are when you return?"

Aim, shoot, bull's-eye. Allison uttered the very questions he'd feared the judge determining his custody status would ask. But it wasn't a fair question. When deployed, men and women missed births, holidays, recitals, and other large chunks of their children's lives, but they still served. And he was damn good at his job. He was no miracle worker but years at the controls is what kept a cool head and saved lives.

"I will do everything humanly possible to provide for my daughter as will the rest of my family."

"The rest of your family are not her parents."

"And neither are you." He shot back calmly. She hadn't said as much, but he wasn't stupid. Why else would she be here?

"I know." Her gaze dropped to her lap and her voice came out so low he barely heard her.

When her eyes lifted to meet his again he saw a sadness that clutched at his heart. He hated to see a woman cry. There was something in a man's DNA that would urge him to move heaven and earth if it would dry a woman's tears. When she blinked and the sadness gave way to determination he breathed more easily. He could fight angry, stubborn, mean and even stupid, but not a crying woman. Not this one.

The overhead bell by the front door sounded and all heads turned to see Brooks and Toni come to stand in the doorway. Ethan hadn't put out a family alert so he wasn't sure if Brooks had arrived for moral support or was simply here because his wife helped Meg with the cooking and baking for the guests.

Brooks' gaze shifted from Ethan to Catherine and the additional serious face in the room. His eyes narrowed briefly and then he glanced up as Meg hurried into the room.

"I tried calling you," Meg told Toni.

"Oh, did you?" Toni pulled her phone from her purse, sighed and nodded. "Forgot to take it off silent." With a hand on her belly, she glanced back at Meg and noticed Ethan, Catherine and Allison watching her.

"Sorry," Ethan said, waving from one person to the other he made quick introductions. Handshakes went all around. Just as Brooks reached out to Allison, Ethan added, "Allison is Francine's sister."

Brooks froze mid-handshake and glanced to Catherine. She nodded. The increased tension in the room was palpable.

"Brooks is a doctor also," Ethan added in an effort to put everyone more at ease.

"I believe I read something about that," Allison retrieved her hand and offered a slight smile. A polite company sort of smile. "Dallas, right?"

"Not for a long time." Brooks grabbed his wife's hand. "I'm the old doc in these parts."

Allison's polite smile held, but the stiffness in her shoulders eased slightly. "You don't miss the big city?"

"Not even a little. I learned the hard way you can take the boy out of the country but you can't take the country out of the boy."

Chuckling, Allison relaxed more fully in her seat. "I've worked with a few of you."

"Where do you call home?"

"Northern California. Bay area. Did my time at San Francisco General and then Stanford."

"Stanford," Brooks repeated, his eyes narrowing slightly as he took in her face again. "Monroe?"

Allison nodded, her expression guarded.

"Any relation to the Monroe who's changing prenatal surgery

since separating conjoined twins last year?"

A hint of rose tinted her cheeks. "That would be me."

Brooks' eyes rounded, and clearly forgetting her connection to Francine and his niece, and everyone else in the room, pulled up the nearest chair and began shooting medical questions at the woman Ethan had been certain until five minutes ago was here to steal his daughter. With every smile, and laugh, and the brilliant intensity with which her eyes beamed as she and Brooks exchanged information, no matter what his lawyer and sister-in-law told him, for the first time Ethan had the sinking feeling that losing his daughter might not be such a long shot.

CHAPTER TEN

"I really appreciate you ladies coming out here instead of to the café," Eileen said as she dealt another round of cards.

Hairpins between her teeth, Ruth Ann spun her long hair into a bun and, talking through her teeth, jabbed the knot of hair onto the top of her head. "I say it's a crazy idea."

Sally May fanned the cards in her hand. "Maybe. Maybe not."

"I'll open." Dorothy tossed a chip into the brass dish. Whenever they played cards at the café the chips were tossed into a pile in the middle of the table. At the ranch they always used the tarnished old bowl that reminded Eileen of a sawed off spittoon.

"Will you give a gal a chance to see what she's got?" Sally May shook her head and shifted the cards around.

"Not me." Ruth Ann put her cards down. "I couldn't even play Go Fish with this hand."

"I don't suppose that niece of yours dropped off some of those delicious cake balls?" Dorothy tossed a chip into the pot. "I'm in."

"Are you kidding?" Eileen laughed. "Sean would sooner let me set the barn on fire before he'd let us near those booze balls again."

Grace kicked the boot cleaner and walked into the kitchen. "Every time I come home and agree to help Dad and Finn I remember why I go to law school."

"You love it and you know it," Eileen called over her shoulder. Every one of her nephews had left the ranch to see the world and live a little. One by one they'd all started coming home. Deep down she prayed every day that Ethan and Grace would find their happiness close to home like the others.

"No one loves mucking stalls and shoveling manure." Grace washed her hands in the sink.

"How's Stacy coming along?" Sally May tossed down two cards.

"The kid's a natural. If there's such a thing as a horseman gene, she's got it just like her mom and her grandmom." Grace filled a glass of water and took a long swallow. "I will admit, I'm having fun teaching her everything I know."

"And some day you can do that for Brittany too," Aunt Eileen added.

Grace downed the last of the water and moved over to the card table set up to one side of the dining room. "By then Stacy will be able to teach her. How come y'all are playing here and not at the café?"

"I wanted to be here if Ethan needed me this morning," Eileen said. Besides, she didn't want every busybody in town eavesdropping on what she had to say.

Grace looked up and listened for the sounds of a playful baby. "Where is she?"

"Catherine picked Ethan and the baby up a little while ago and took them into town to meet the aunt."

Grace's face crinkled unpleasantly. "I thought we were going to wait until we heard from the judge?"

"Nope." Eileen shook her head. "The lawyers, including Catherine, agreed that if we play nice it will look better to a court than if we try and keep her away."

"Which is why you want to move her in here?" Dorothy picked up her new cards.

"Are you mad?" Grace spat.

Eileen shook her head. "You may look like your mama but you sure do sound like your father."

"Because Dad is a smart man."

"Maybe," Eileen shrugged, "when it comes to cattle and ranches and sons."

"I'm with her." Ruth Ann reached down and scratched the

dog comfortably planted between her and Sally May. "What do you expect to gain from bringing the woman here?"

Sally May looked over the edge of her cards at their friend.

"When did you grow so old?" Dorothy asked.

"I'm not old," Ruth Ann shot back.

Dorothy shook her head. "Are you needing a refresher course on the birds and the bees?"

"Not all birds fall for all bees." Ruth Ann looked from one friend to the other. "It's a long shot that might blow up in your face."

"I don't think so." Eileen smiled confidently.

Grace shook her head, grabbed a slice of cheese and a cracker from the nearby tray and leaned over to kiss her aunt on the cheek. "I love you, but you're nuts. Please don't do anything that will make things worse." Straightening, she spun on her heel. "I'm going to catch a shower and change. I'll let you ladies talk some sense into her."

"Whatever you say, dear."

From the hall Grace called back, "You behave or I'm going to tell Daddy you're up to something."

Eileen shook her head and waited until Grace's steps faded down the upstairs hall then leaned forward. "Did I tell you how they first met?"

"In the café," Dorothy said.

"Nope." Eileen set her cards face down on the table and looked at each of her friends. "A furry gray dog introduced them."

"*The* dog?" Sally May dropped her hands to the table, almost forgetting to turn her cards face down.

"Well." Eileen picked her cards back up. "Probably not."

"Why probably not?" Ruth Ann asked.

"They were in California at the time."

Both Sally May's and Dorothy's hands fell to the table, concealing their cards from view a forgotten cause. Ruth Ann stared at her, slack jawed.

Dorothy spoke first. "Your family is right. You've lost your mind."

"You can't seriously believe there's a matchmaking dog running around the country marrying off your nephews?" Sally May said.

Ruth Ann shook her head. "Are you sure your niece hasn't been slipping you an overdose of booze balls?"

"What I need, ladies, is a little bit of social club ingenuity. I've got a red blooded though slightly gimpy nephew and an attractive smart woman with two things in common—my niece and a shaggy dog. All I need is a plan to help nature run its course."

• • • •

What was the point? Allison threw off the covers and sprang to her feet with the force of a woman running from a burning bed. She'd tossed and turned enough to have carved a rut in the luxury bed. The clock on the nightstand flashed 10 a.m. She shouldn't have bothered going back to sleep.

Unable to really sleep, at two o'clock in the morning she'd pulled out her laptop and attempted to update some requested reports. "Attempt" being the key word. Reading incoming medical jargon instead hadn't gone over any better, and she'd finally settled for catching up on the emails she'd ignored for almost two days. By six in the morning she'd made another effort at getting some sleep before Ethan, Catherine and baby Brittany arrived.

The occasional visions of Francine and her in happier days blended with nightmarish scenarios that, in order to maintain her own sanity, Allison had long ago learned to bury deep in the back of her mind. The odd mixture sprinted back and forth from a semi-conscious state until Allison climbed out of bed feeling more exhausted now than she had when she'd gone to bed the night before. Standing in front of her open suitcase, she picked up a blouse. What did a woman wear to meet her niece for the first time?

A rap at the door dragged her attention away from her

wardrobe.

"Knock knock," Meg said softly through the closed door.

"Come in."

Juggling a full tray, her hostess shoved the door open. "Since you missed breakfast, thought you might like a little something before Ethan gets here."

A carafe, a teapot, an empty mug, a plate of mixed fruit, a muffin, another dish with scrambled eggs and bacon, and a glass of orange juice all bumped up against each other covering every available inch of space. "I thought you said you don't cook?"

Meg set the tray down and smiled. "You were listening."

"It's a key element of my job." She reached for a strip of bacon. "Sometimes the only way to uncover what is really wrong with a patient is to read between the lines and listen to what they're not telling you."

"I see." Meg took a step back. "I didn't know if you'd prefer coffee in the morning so there's coffee in the glass carafe and tea in the pot. The muffins are homemade so I'd make sure to at least have a taste. If there's something you might like that I didn't think of, just whistle."

"This is very nice of you." Allison bit into the bacon.

"We aim to please. Besides, I'd hate to have you leave us a bad review."

The twinkle in Meg's eyes at the comment made Allison laugh in earnest. She'd needed the release. "I don't know why I'm so scared."

"Because Brittany is important to you."

Allison nodded. A lot of things were becoming important.

The rumble of an engine carried up to the room and Meg immediately glanced toward the window. Her eyes blinking, she made a slight hissing sound and turned back around. "You may have to skip the coffee. They're here."

"Now?" Allison ran to the window. A massive pickup truck with four doors came to a stop in front of the house. "He's early!"

"Take a breath," Meg said slowly. "I'll keep everyone happy

till you're ready."

"Ready. Right." Allison looked at her suitcase again.

"Brittany won't care what you wear. This is casual country. A pair of jeans will be fine."

"If I'd brought a pair."

"Then whatever. Stop worrying." Meg gently patted her arm. "See you downstairs."

Allison nodded. "Thanks."

The bedroom door closed and Allison was alone and about to put the fast art of washing and dressing before the fire-heated water ran cold into practice in that glorious bathroom. In less than fifteen minutes she was downstairs and following the voices into the kitchen.

"Good morning." Ethan must have heard her steps because he was on his feet by the time she turned the corner.

"Please sit down."

Ethan bobbed his head and leaned back onto the stool.

Allison was all set to tell him about elevating his leg when she spotted the baby in Meg's arms. "Oh my."

"Looks who's here," Meg said to the baby in a soft lilt. "It's your aunt Allison."

Without thinking, Allison crossed the room to where Francine's little girl was, but before extending her arms to the baby, she instinctively turned to Ethan. He gave her a quick nod and the next thing she knew she was looking into laughing green eyes.

"She likes you," Meg said. "Why don't you two go sit out on the back porch? I've got a few things to take care of. When Catherine returns for you after her errands, I'll fix us some lunch."

Ethan nodded and waited for her to lead the way. On the porch she turned. The man, tall as a small tree with eyes so green they reminded her of the marbles her neighbor collected as a kid, used muscles strong enough to swing all six-foot-plus of him on crutches across the house with the ease of a man with two good feet.

Forest green rockers lined the outdoor seating area. She picked the one closest to the door and eased into it, swaying back and forth with Brittany in her arms. "You are too sweet." The baby latched onto a finger and Allison felt her cheeks pull into a wide smile. She turned to share the moment with the only other person around and slammed into that blasted unreadable face. Ethan would have made a great Beefeater standing guard at Buckingham Palace.

Ethan picked one of two wicker chairs that didn't rock. Facing her, with the arm of his crutch he hooked and dragged a side table around to prop his leg on. "Just so you don't have to fight the urge to tell me to raise my leg."

"I didn't say anything."

"No, but you were thinking it."

She bit back a smile and turned her attention again to her niece. Happy green eyes twinkled at her. "You're as pretty as your mama." Again she glanced at Ethan, and was surprised to see his expression had softened. Whether it was at the baby or the mention of Francine, she didn't know.

Sitting the baby on her knees, Allison jiggled her legs up and down, making Brittany bounce and giggle.

"I didn't know she likes that." Ethan actually smiled.

"Most babies do. They love movement."

"You're good with her."

"Thank you." Allison opened her eyes and mouth wide a few times and Brittany's face lit up with amusement. "They really are easy to entertain at this age. I think she has your eyes."

Ethan looked surprised.

"Francine's are more blue." Allison stopped bouncing her legs and faced Ethan. "Did you love her?"

He shook his head. There was no moment of hesitation, no contemplation, consideration, just a movement of his head from left to right and back.

Allison began bouncing again, keeping her eyes on the baby. She shouldn't have felt relieved. "How long were you together?"

"A few days."

Her knees stopped and her head whipped around to face him. At least he had the decency to look contrite. Not that it was his fault her sister slept with men she couldn't possibly know well.

"I did like her."

That was something, she supposed.

"And I'd have been there for her, as much as I could, if I'd known she was pregnant."

Studying him a moment, she saw sincerity in his eyes. "So she never tried to contact you before…" She couldn't say "before she'd abandoned her baby" out loud.

Ethan shook his head again. "Not a word." With his good hand he began rubbing the side of his broken leg. At the same time the thumb on his injured hand rubbed across the tips of his fingers. He had to be uncomfortable.

Allison shifted her niece so she could play with her fingers and see her daddy. "I don't understand how she could walk away like she did."

"I stopped trying to understand. A different question haunts me."

Looking up, she met his gaze. "What's that?"

"Is Fancy going to come back?"

CHAPTER ELEVEN

Several things crossed Ethan's mind. When the time came, would he be allowed to do physical therapy for his leg and hand in Butler Springs to stay near Brittany or would he need to return to home base? How would having a dependent affect his performance? He'd seen it before, the best SEALs, Rangers, and jet jocks lose their edge once they were worried about making a wife a widow or a child an orphan. But right now he mostly wondered, could he do right by this precious little girl? He leaned forward and brushed the back of his knuckle against Brittany's cheek and she rewarded him with a huge gurgling smile. "That's my girl."

Allison's expression shifted.

He wasn't sure exactly what he was reading—hell, he was as bad at reading a woman's mind as he was good at flying his helo—but if he had to guess he'd venture a wave of sadness or maybe melancholy, or could it be longing that crossed her face? "Do you want children?"

Her face lifted to his and her eyes moved about as though searching for the answer in the distance. "I didn't think so."

"Didn't or don't?"

"I'm not sure." She lifted Brittany up high so her feet dangled and then Allison made munching sounds as she pretended to nibble on Brittany's toes. After a couple of repeats, she set the baby back on her lap and this time he was sure it was longing he saw in her eyes. "I guess I do."

"For what it's worth, looks to me like you'd be good at the job."

A sweet smile crossed her lips and a hint of pink tinged her cheeks. He liked the way she blushed when paid a compliment.

She'd done it a couple of times as Brooks gushed over her accomplishments last night, but Ethan had noticed the blush came more when the praise was personal.

Her fingers trapped in Brittany's grip, the baby shifted from deep examination to the occasional tasting and Allison cast her gaze to a distant point in the yard. "We didn't have the ideal upbringing. My parents traveled a lot when we were little, but I remember Mum being caring and gentle when they were home. I was only eight when they were killed in a plane crash. Fancy was almost twelve."

"You call her Fancy?" He'd thought it was a nickname Francine had chosen to avoid giving her real name.

A smile teased at one side of her mouth. "I couldn't say Francine when I was little. Even though my mother detested it, my dad called her Franny. Somehow I came up with a combination of both and she got dubbed Fancy. I'm not sure which name mother disliked more."

"Your mom liked the name she'd chosen." Made sense to him. Southerners were notorious for saddling cute little kids with massively long names like Jefferson Beauregard or Abigail Elizabeth and frowning if any human being dared call the child anything less than their full Christian name.

"Mum was English. I think it ruffled her natural sensibilities."

"I gather your father was not?"

"Born and bred Yankee." She wiggled her fingers at the baby's tummy. "Dad didn't have any living family so we went to live with my Aunt Millicent after the accident. She was an antique dealer in Boston. She was completely out of her depth with us. I know she loved us, but she'd come from a mindset of children should be seen and not heard. She expected us to be little adults. It didn't go well. I was able to lose myself in my books. I guess you could call me the brainiac. Fancy wasn't very academically inclined. Another sore spot with my aunt. The best times we had were when she went on a long buying trip and left us with the housekeeper."

He'd never asked Fancy how old she was, but now that he thought about it Allison looked awfully young to be as accomplished a physician as Brooks made her out to be. "So you were smart?"

"Skipped second grade and then fourth. By then my aunt was already having trouble with Francine—"

"Until now I hadn't realized you're younger than your sister."

Allison nodded. "Which was why my aunt decided my being the youngest in my class wasn't in my best interest. Instead she moved me to a more structured college prep for girls."

"Structured." Code word for hard ass. "How did that go?"

"Fine, I suppose. I liked books. They didn't care if I was younger or smarter than they were. I graduated at sixteen, got a scholarship to Stanford, and took it."

"Getting away from the aunt?"

Allison blinked at him. "I, uh, hadn't considered that." She shook her head. "A postcard had come to my aunt's house from Francine the year before telling us she'd gotten married and was happy in sunny California. Aunt Millicent wanted me to go to Harvard. I wanted to be closer to Francine, just in case she reached out to me again. Maybe deep down, like my sister, I wanted to get as geographically far away from New England too."

"The mind is an interesting thing."

This time Allison smiled. "I almost became a psychiatrist. Trying to understand what went wrong with my sister, what could I have done differently to make things better—"

"Like the child of divorce who thinks their parents behavior is their fault." His heart ached for the hurt child she must have been. "You were just a kid yourself. Nothing anyone could have done."

"I know that here," she tapped her temple, "but here," she tapped her heart, "not so much."

"So you passed on psychiatry?"

She chuckled. "Let go of the mind but couldn't quite let go of the brain. I started my residency in neurology. I suppose I still needed to understand how the brain worked. Wanted to be the best brain surgeon ever—"

"Brooks could have used you if you had."

"Why is that?" she frowned.

"Kid we grew up with moved away for college, got married, and recently moved back, but he was a changed man."

"In what way?"

"As a boy he was the kindest, gentlest soul. When he moved home he was aggressive, short tempered and my brother's wife Toni was the first to notice signs of physical abuse with his wife."

"A tumor?" she mumbled.

"Yeah, but no one suspected it soon enough. I think Brooks blames himself for that."

"Nonsense. I know some of the most skilled neurologists in the world who don't recognize a tumor until a PET scan points it out."

"That's pretty much what happened, except due to recent events, the guy may wind up in jail if the doctors can't convince a judge his behavior was caused by the tumor."

"Well that shouldn't be hard."

"You'd think. I'm not fully aware of the issues, but in a nutshell the tumor is in a delicate place, not the sort of thing surgeons in Butler Springs are known for, and it's complicated because he's a prisoner in the court system. For now, he's undergoing some treatment in an effort to shrink the tumor, and his criminal future is sketchy."

Allison nodded with each sentence. "Maybe I can help."

"You do brain surgery or do you have a Texas judge in your family tree?"

She chuckled again. "No brain surgery and no judges. But I've got some great contacts. I'll get with Brooks later today, get a more detailed report. See if I can help."

"Thanks. That would be appreciated. I've not met our friend's wife but she's got the whole town looking out for her. You do a lot of volunteer work, don't you?"

She nodded again. "Both home and overseas."

"Paying penance?"

Her eyes flew open wide. "No. I like helping."

Altruism was not a difficult concept to swallow. Ethan flew into some crazy dangerous places under miserable circumstances because he liked being the good guy. He liked knowing his family could go to the grocery store or drive down the road without fear or concerns that some nutcase who wanted to meet seventy-two virgins was going to blow them to pieces. That they could go to church on Sundays and say grace at the dinner table without fear of retribution. But he also liked the thrill of flying, the thrill of beating the odds, and wondered if the monkey on Allison's back wasn't still trying to right what went so wrong in her own sister so many years ago.

• • • •

After playing nicely with no distraction other than her aunt's long fingers and occasional interactions, Brittany let out the first signs of a fussy nature. "Uh oh," Allison stood and looked to Ethan. "Diaper, hungry or tired?"

Ethan grabbed his crutches and stood as well. "Could be hungry or wet. Even tired she doesn't really fuss, she just rubs her eyes or tugs at her ear and settles in for a nap wherever she is."

"Okay. Then should we start with the diaper or a bottle?"

"I'd go with bottle. She does seem to have a pretty healthy appetite for a baby. Diaper bag is in the kitchen." Ethan led the way back into the house.

"You get around pretty good on those."

He unzipped the bag on the counter and pulled out a premade bottle. "I'd rather be walking." His gaze darted over to the microwave. "Would you mind?"

"Not at all." Accepting the bottle, she crossed the room. "How long?"

"Twenty seconds is enough."

"It has to be frustrating." Baby in one arm, she waited for the timer to ding.

"I don't care about the crutches. I've got plenty of upper body strength. A few weeks on these is a piece of cake compared to regular PT. It's not being able to walk with her, push her in a stroller, carry the bottle to the microwave."

"How's diaper duty?"

"Not bad if it's only wet, otherwise my fine motor skills need improvement."

She chuckled and retrieved the bottle. "I can see that. Shall we head to the living room with the more comfortable chairs?"

Ethan nodded at her and even on crutches with an injured hand he still beat her into the other room.

"You really are good on those."

He shrugged.

"Something tells me you're good at a lot of things." She hadn't meant anything untoward by the statement, but the way the corner of his lips tipped up and his eyes twinkled, she had the feeling that was exactly where his mind had gone. Having spent most of her life studying or working rather than socializing, her *faux-pas* filter didn't always work, and damned if she didn't feel the embarrassed flush rushing to her cheeks.

"You're awfully cute when you blush."

"Oh Lord." She wanted to crawl under the nearest rock. Thirty-one years old and the nicest thing a good looking man can say is she's cute. And why? Because she still blushed with the ease of a virtuous teenager? "I'm not a virgin."

Ethan's eyes widened in surprise and then twinkled with amusement. "Um, no, I, uh, wouldn't guess you were."

Now she seriously wanted to hide in a corner. Why the hell did she say that out loud? And what else was he supposed to say now. "Do you want to feed her or shall I?"

He smiled sweetly at her lame attempt to avoid the dumb bomb she'd dropped. "Would you like to?"

"Yes. Yes, I would." Besides needing the distraction, something to do with her hands and someplace else to look besides into those gorgeous twinkling green eyes, she really did want to connect with her little niece more than she'd realized. With the sweet bundle cradled in her arms, Allison forgot all about her verbal blunder, and the frustration she felt every time anyone pointed out how young she was or how inexperienced.

Brittany sucked away, her hand resting on Allison's fingers. Her heart swelled in her chest, almost robbing her of breath. She worked with babies day in and day out. Nothing escaped her when it came to understanding just how miraculous every healthy baby was, but this was her own flesh and blood, the closest thing to her own child on this planet. The reality was mind boggling. As was the connection this child had formed with her father. As fascinated as Brittany was with the new face playing with her and feeding her, every few seconds she'd look across to where her father sat.

Ethan must have noticed too. "I'm usually the only one who feeds her in the daytime."

Another lump formed in her chest. Only a few weeks and daughter and father had bonded. "She loves you already."

"I love her. I didn't fathom how much I could love another human being. Don't really understand why it's any different than how much I love the rest of my family, but it is. Different, I mean."

Allison nodded. "Yes, I bet it is."

What would be in her niece's best interest didn't seem so glaringly obvious to her any more. So what the hell was she supposed to do now?

CHAPTER TWELVE

"If your aunt finds out I let you drive she's going to take out one of those rifles and shoot me," Catherine said.

"Nonsense." Ethan tightened his grip on the steering wheel. It had taken some convincing and a little demonstration that he could indeed drive the pickup with his left foot, but he desperately needed to feel in control of something for a little bit. Even if it was only the truck on the ride home. "Aunt Eileen wants more Farradays and she already knows you can procreate. You're perfectly safe."

"Safe isn't the first word that comes to mind." Catherine leaned back in the passenger seat and crossed her arms. "We are going to stop outside the ranch and switch places."

"Chicken."

"Survival instinct," she deadpanned and then smiled.

Ethan laughed. Of the new women in the Farraday family he knew Catherine the least. Not that he'd known the others much better, but at least he'd been home for Adam's wedding and gotten a chance to get to know Meg and Toni. Catherine joined the picture after Ethan had returned to the sandbox. Over the last twenty-four hours he'd come to know her a lot better, between battling for Brittany and driving back and forth to the ranch. No wonder his brother loved her. Two spitfires. "Did you two decide on a date finally?"

"The date wasn't the problem."

"That's right. Vegas versus Aunt Eileen."

Catherine laughed. "I don't believe Vegas was ever mentioned. At least not in earnest."

"No. I'm pretty sure when my brother said he'd be happy putting you in a car and not stopping till he found a preacher in

Vegas, he wasn't kidding." Ethan took his gaze from the road and looked Catherine in the eyes. "You do realize just how much my brother wants to make you his wife?" From the face splitting grin that took over, Ethan was pretty sure she did and that the feeling was very mutual. "So where's the problem?"

"There isn't a problem. I've been married before in an elaborate celebration to rival the royal wedding. I don't need that again."

"But Aunt Eileen wants it?" He'd thought that every woman wanted a big, splashy wedding but he hadn't thought that Catherine had already been there, done that.

"I know Connor doesn't care for a big wedding any more than I do. But with Brooks having had such a small private ceremony, making a fuss seems to mean a great deal to your aunt."

He loved that his aunt's feelings were as important to Catherine as to all of his siblings.

"We just needed for Becky and DJ to start making plans."

"I'm confused. Why?"

"Because Becky has never been married. She's that sugar and spice and everything nice kind of gal who probably envisioned every detail of her wedding from the moment she hit puberty."

Ethan bit his tongue. Catherine was probably right, but there was no point in bringing up that those plans had most likely included him and not DJ. At least until recently.

"Don't get all nostalgic on me." Catherine shot him a pointed glare. "You were a crush, DJ is the love of her life and Becky deserves all the fun and hoopla that's going to go with two townfolk tying the knot. Now that Aunt Eileen can get carried away planning the wedding of the year with her best friend, she's more reasonable about a smaller wedding for us. Not as private as Brooks but not the society event of the year either."

"So what you're saying is…"

Catherine smiled. "Hopefully before you have to leave. Four weeks from today."

If he weren't on the road Ethan would have pulled her into a "welcome to the family" bear-squishing hug. "I may still be hobbling, but I'll be there."

"You should be in a walking boot soon, right?"

He nodded. "Should be." He also might be on his way to Pendleton again. So much more was yet to be decided besides wedding dates for his brothers who were dropping like flies in a sugar coma. "Do you think the judge will have approved the release of rights by then?"

"It's a possibility."

"You're worried about Allison?" He chanced a glance in her direction.

"Not really. In the end she doesn't have a leg to stand on if she wants to interfere with your custody of Brittany. It's just that things could drag on awkwardly if she decides to pursue any legal action."

Ethan squeezed the steering wheel again, yearning to feel the cool hard surface under both his hands. "So you think she's going to do something?"

"I don't know. You've spent more time with her today than all of us combined. What do you think she wants?"

And wasn't that an interesting question. Yesterday he would have said hands down that she wanted custody of Brittany. Today, he wasn't so sure. The look on her face showed that she was already in love with the little girl. And he didn't doubt she was hoping for custody, but he wondered if she wasn't really after something else. Something humanly impossible. Saving a family that never really was.

• • • •

Some things made no sense in life. It was the hardest thing for Allison to accept. As a doctor she wanted black and white answers to everything. Good or bad. But life had a way of handing out nothing but shades of gray. For the last few hours since Ethan and Brittany had left, she'd made a serious effort at work. The little emergency patient who had delayed her departure for Texas was doing what came naturally, healing fast and well. Allison reached out to Brooks Farraday about his tumor patient and he'd immediately jumped at the chance for a renowned opinion. From the sound of it, all the Farradays and half the town would jump through a hoop of fire to help their friend. She liked that idea.

Movies, books, and folklore touted the glories of small town living. Allison was pretty sure she'd never believed any of it. Human nature was too flawed for an Ozzie and Harriet lifestyle. She was beginning to rethink that philosophy.

When she'd showed up downstairs looking to clear her thoughts, Meg had offered to fix her a snack. Had Meg not been so close to the problem, Allison would have relished a chance to talk out her situation. As it was, she was having a hard time understanding why Meg and Adam were being so nice to her. If this had been the movie of the week, there would be plots and treachery around every corner scheming to run her out of town on a rail.

For all she knew maybe there *was* scheming and plotting about how to get rid of her once and for all, and the friendly banter and sweet smiles were all a pleasant façade. A Trojan horse. Though she doubted it seriously. No, instead of talking off her hostess' ear, Allison found herself walking up Main Street on her way to the old café. This time she was able to take in the shops along the way. For a few minutes she peered inside the Cut and Curl, fascinated by the line of old hairdryers along the back wall. Scenes from some of her favorite movies depicting women in the fifties gossiping under the huge metallic contraptions flittered through her mind.

Not far along, the shop named *Sisters* caught her eye. The window display held an array of varied items from women's shoes to baby layettes. It was the infant products that pulled her inside. An old fashioned merchant bell sounded as the door opened and closed.

Immediately a smiling, short and rounded blonde with a

bouffant hairdo worthy of those movies Allison had just been reminiscing about, appeared in front of her. "You must be one of Meg's guests. Welcome to Tuckers Bluff."

"Yes, I am. Thank you." The woman's smile was infectious.

Before Allison could say anything else a tall, slim strawberry blonde came hurrying out from behind a curtain. "Oh, hello. I didn't hear the bell. Is Sister helping you find what you want?"

"We haven't gotten that far yet, Sissy. The lady just walked in the door."

"Well." The tall woman smiled. "How can we help you?"

Allison glanced around the deceptively large store and her gaze settled on a small section of baby furniture. "I'd like to get a gift for a baby."

"Ooh," the shorter one slapped her hands together and rubbed enthusiastically. "We love babies. How old?"

"Just a few months." Allison should have been able to do the math quickly in her head, but she'd drawn a blank. What kind of aunt did that make her not knowing Brittany's age to the day?

"Girl or boy?" the taller one asked, already walking to the area of the store that had caught Allison's eye.

"Girl."

The two women glanced at each other a moment. One raised a brow, the other made a funny face with her mouth and then they both shrugged. Sister and Sissy. They didn't look a blessed thing like siblings and yet they communicated with the ease of identical twins.

"She's a very happy baby." Allison felt a need to prove she did know something about her niece, even though these ladies had no idea what her situation was. Or did they? This was, after all, a small town. But surely it wasn't *that* small.

"Is she sitting up on her own?" Sissy asked.

Allison drew another blank. Most babies didn't sit until they were at least six months old and transitional sitting on their own happened closer to eight months, but that was merely a guidepost. Her mind quickly scrolled through the moments of watching and playing with the baby and couldn't remember a single time when she'd been put down to sit. "No."

"Okay, her bottom hasn't flattened out yet."

"Excuse me?"

The two sisters laughed. "That's what we say when a baby is too young to sit. Their bottom hasn't flattened out yet so they fall over."

"Oh." That was a term they'd failed to teach her in medical school, but she supposed it worked as well as any physiological explanation she could have come up with. "She seems fascinated with grabbing my fingers."

"Okay. Does she have a good rattle?"

Again, Allison didn't have a quick answer. She had little idea of what the child had other than the few things in her diaper bag and no toys had been produced. "I don't think so."

The two sisters paused to look at each other and Sissy turned back to face her. "Are you visiting a family here in Tuckers Bluff?"

Finally a question Allison could answer quickly and confidently. "Yes. The Farradays."

"Oh," the two women echoed.

"You're visiting little Brittany. Sweetest child." Sissy began moving small boxes from atop a nearby table. "Why, from the day DJ and Becky walked in here she stole our hearts."

"And the whole town's too," Sister added, a slight frown pinching her brows. "Makes my blood boil every time I think what that mama did."

"Now, Sister." Sissy opened a box and slid the lid back on. "Leaving that child with her papa and uncles was the best thing for that baby. No place better to raise a child than here in Tuckers Bluff."

"Or with the Farradays. Such good people." Sister bobbed her head. "That Aunt Eileen, giving up her own life, her fiancé, and staying here to raise her sister's children. She did Helen proud."

"Yes sirree. We've got some mighty fine families. Here it is."

Sissy waved a colorful small box. "Ever since they moved Brittany into the ranch house and got her her own room we've sold through just about every baby item we had."

"That we have," the plump sister agreed.

"But this here isn't made in China or some other heathen country."

"Sissy!"

"I know. I'm sorry. Just gets my goat every time I think of all the jobs this country has lost. We came this close," she pinched her fingers close together, "to having a blue jean factory in the county twenty years ago. Would have been a big boost to the town. Kept more of our young folk here," the thin woman sighed. "Anyhow, this," she held up the box, "was handmade and the wood stained with natural colors so nothing toxic to hurt the baby. Just the right size for little Brittany's hands."

The sister shook the tiny rattle, smiled, and handed it off to Allison. The light weight surprised her. And from what she could tell the pieces were carved and fit together like a fine piece of dovetailed furniture. The round bulb that made the noises was a pale shade of red. The handle grip a lighter deep blue and the ring at the bottom a pretty yellow.

"Perfectly safe for chewing and slobbering on too."

"It's lovely." Allison had never seen such a simple yet lovely piece. "Do we know who made it?"

The sisters did that eye contact thing again.

"Local rancher. He likes to work with wood. This is the only rattle he ever made. Told us it had to go to someone special." Sissy handed Allison the small box it had come in. "I know Brittany fits the requirement. Maybe you do too."

CHAPTER THIRTEEN

"I will bloody be damned." Brooks walked into the living room with his wife at his side. "She did it."

"Who did what?" Aunt Eileen peeked at the roast in the oven.

"Allison. She forwarded Jake's files to an associate of hers at Stanford. Not any associate. The number two brain surgeon in the country."

"And?" Ethan coaxed. The way Brooks was bouncing out of his skin there had to be more.

"And he's agreed to do Jake's surgery. He's also agreed to send a report to the judge on a recent compilation of case studies for post surgery violence on exactly this type of tumor."

Aunt Eileen closed the oven door. "I wouldn't have thought there were that many cases to do a qualified report."

"More than we'd think. He's going to do his work pro-bono, but the hospital, transport and other things are going to cost a pretty penny."

"Who's paying for it?" Connor asked.

"Old man Thomas."

All movement in the house froze as though some omniscient being had struck the pause button on a remote control.

Sean Farraday looked from son to son. "Any father would."

"Not old man Thomas." Ethan may have been gone more often than not through the years, but old man Thomas' reputation followed him everywhere. "That man never spent a dime on his family that could have been spent on a horse."

"Do you think he's going to sell some of the horses?" Connor asked.

"Not likely." Their father shook his head

"No," Brooks shrugged. "It's just rumor, but he might be putting the feed store up for sale."

Aunt Eileen stopped by Brooks' side. "That could take a while."

"You think anyone from town would want to take it on?" Grace asked.

Sean Farraday shook his head. "Can't think of someone with that kind of money or the time for it."

"What about one of the Bradys?" Aunt Eileen moved toward the sink. "They're an awfully big clan and the family land is spreading thinner and thinner with each generation."

"Maybe," Sean Farraday agreed. "I guess you never know."

"Maybe some outsider will bring in new business." Grace set the knives and forks around the table then came to the end and paused. "We have one place setting too many."

"No we don't." Aunt Eileen turned the kitchen faucet on.

Grace counted the settings. "Who's the fourteenth place?"

"Which reminds me," Eileen glanced over her shoulder at her brother-in-law. "With the family growing so fast, we're going to need a bigger table. Thought maybe you might like to make that your next project."

Sean Farraday looked at the table he'd made for his wife after Finn was born. Helen Farraday had been thinking ahead when she'd had her husband extend the dining room out onto what used to be a wraparound porch. It was no surprise to anyone that now their aunt was thinking ahead too. Sean didn't say a word, just nodded at his sister-in-law and she smiled in return. They'd done a lot of that type of communicating through the years. It had always made Ethan wonder if that's the way his mom would have communicated too.

"Which still leaves the question, who is this last place for?" Grace repeated.

Aunt Eileen turned off the water and spun about to face her niece. "I've invited Allison to join us for Sunday supper."

Eight heads turned from person to person. Not a single one

dared to argue with the family matriarch. And truthfully, Ethan was sort of glad she had.

• • • •

Allison pulled into the long drive behind Meg and Adam. They'd offered to give her a ride, but she'd wanted the freedom of her own car in case the situation became too awkward and she needed to return to the B&B.

Set back in the distance, the ranch house stood out like a picture postcard for an old western. From a few minutes outside of town until now there hadn't been a blessed sign of life. Over breakfast Adam and Meg had chatted about living in West Texas. Another guest had asked a good many questions about the ranch, and Allison had listened eagerly in silence. There were a lot of details that could be had by checking the almighty Google, but she'd learned so much more at the table.

Even though Adam never revealed any details about how many head of cattle they ran, or what the government paid them to keep the wild horses, she'd still been left with a pretty solid picture of exactly how well off the Farraday ranch was. Not only did she learn about how many acres of land it took to feed cattle in this dryer part of the state, she also ascertained a good deal about Connor and the horse operation he'd started with his fiancée, the lawyer.

Now that she was pulling up to the famed ranch in living color, she had a sneaking suspicion that a good chunk of the land they'd driven through to get here had been Farraday country. With every new trickle of information, she saw her chances at bringing her niece home with her slipping further and further away. Even after researching the family before her trip, she'd still hoped to find a gung-ho marine with little or no interest in raising a daughter. The only time she'd recently felt the slightest bit of hope was when Ethan spoke of returning to active duty. She could see in his eyes how much he loved what he did for the military. That was her ace in the hole.

Following the line of cars, she parked beside Adam's huge pickup truck. Allison almost laughed out loud the first time she saw it. Apparently the old joke everything's bigger in Texas had more than a grain of truth to it. Adam's wasn't the only truck she'd seen in town large enough to house a small tribe. She wasn't a small woman by any means, but even she'd need a stepladder to climb into that monster, and the tumble on the way out was one hell of a drop.

Gathering her purse, the rattle and the stuffed piggy that was so soft and snuggly she hadn't been able to resist, Allison followed Adam and Meg into the house. The first thing to strike her was the noise level. Loud and a bit raucous with mixtures of laughter and debates and plenty of slamming cabinets and clanking glasses and silverware, the air was alive and kicking with positive energy. Despite the apprehension the day held for her, she couldn't stop herself from smiling.

Crossing the foyer, she glanced right and spotted Ethan on the recliner, his eyes closed, with Brittany sprawled across his broad chest, one hand splayed atop her back, keeping her safely in place. Brittany looked so much tinier against him. Veering away from the direction Meg was taking, Allison stepped slowly into the family den. The sight of father and daughter, the juxtaposition of giant and infant, the impact of protector and innocent gripped Allison's heart and squeezed. How was she supposed to fight that?

Ethan's one eye popped open. "Hello."

"Hi," she whispered. "I thought you were sleeping."

Both eyes open now, one brow rose high on his forehead and with his free hand he pointed his thumb over his shoulder. "With all that racket?"

Allison glanced behind them to the open wall and full view of the family gathered around the kitchen table and realized that she was the only one whispering. "How does she sleep with all this noise?"

Ethan shrugged. "I guess it's whatever you're used to."

Immediately Allison's mind flashed back to how loud the virgin jungles sounded to her at first, making it impossible for her to sleep even a wink, and how by the time she'd left she could have slept through the blitzkrieg. "Makes sense." She lifted the small bag with the gifts. "I brought a little something for her."

One side of his mouth tipped upward followed by the opposite corner and Allison felt the impact of the huge smile all the way to her toes.

"That was nice of you."

"She is my niece."

Brittany wiggled, her tiny fisted hand moving closer to her mouth, and let out a soft contented sigh. Allison liked to think that statement had made Brittany happy. Of course, she'd have also liked her sister to stop roaming the country like a 1960s love child and behave more like a normal family. Her gaze lifted to the people working together in the kitchen. Like a Farraday family.

"I didn't hear you arrive." Aunt Eileen wiped her hands on an apple-patterned apron tied around her waist, and then extended her hands at Allison.

Convinced the woman was reaching for the bag Allison carried, she was caught off guard when the family matriarch pulled her into a welcoming hug.

"So glad you could make it." Aunt Eileen smiled. "You just make yourself comfortable in here and I'll have someone bring you a nice glass of tea."

Feeling a tad dumbfounded, Allison merely nodded. It didn't occur to her until she'd sunk onto the sofa that she didn't like iced tea.

"She likes you."

"Yeah. I gathered." Allison looked to the kitchen and back. "Why?"

Ethan shrugged. "Why not?"

Because I'm here to challenge this crazy happy family.

"Brooks said that you're helping Jake Thomas."

"Not me exactly, but once I took a look at the test results

myself and heard more of the details from Brooks, I couldn't not try to help."

"Allison Monroe," Ethan smiled, "you're a nice person."

Was she? Would a nice person fight a family like this for her niece? Would a nice person even try to take her niece away from a family like this? Lord, with every passing moment things grew more confusing.

Ethan's head tilted to one side, his gaze narrowing. "Is that hard to believe?"

"What?" Allison blinked. "Oh. I, uh, I'm not used to hearing personal compliments."

His eyes shot open wide. "Why the hell not? A beautiful, smart and caring person like you should have compliments coming out the wazoo."

Beautiful? Her? Fancy was the pretty one, she was the smart one. Caring, okay, she wouldn't be a doctor if she didn't care. But beautiful?

"Allison?"

She blinked and looked at Ethan's confused expression. "I was a studious awkward teen in an all-girl school. My first couple of years of college not a whole lot of guys paid attention to the smart, awkward, and jailbait female. I finished my degree in three years and worked twice as hard to prove that I belonged in med school, even if I was only nineteen."

"You were nineteen and in med school?" His eyes shone with incredulity.

She shrugged. "Many countries with stronger secondary education, like England, combine college and medical school starting at nineteen."

"You weren't in England or some other country."

"No. But by the time I finished medical school I'd not only proven I belonged, I'd caught the eye of several important professors. Professional compliments I'm used to."

"So, when did you finally outgrow the awkward stage?"

She shrugged. She'd never be the pretty one. Fancy had the

blonde hair and big blue eyes. Allison was the average sister with above average IQ. The only time Allison wasn't awkward was wearing a lab coat and a stethoscope. "Not sure I ever did."

CHAPTER FOURTEEN

N ever did? Did Allison not look in the mirror? If a guy wasn't careful, in a heartbeat those stormy gray eyes could suck him in and never let him loose. Her cute bashful blush that had gotten under his skin more than once brought out every protective instinct engraved in male DNA. And the few times she'd smiled, really smiled, he could feel the pull in places he had no business feeling a damn thing.

"I've been sent to bring the required social beverage of the south." Grinning, Grace came in carrying a tray with two glasses of tea and set it down on the table in front of Allison. "And in deference to your status of revered house guest, you not only warrant Aunt Eileen's company-only apron, I have to use the tray to carry two glasses that would have arrived more easily each in a hand."

"Thank you. But I could have come and gotten them." Allison did that blush thing again and Ethan figured he was going to need every drop of the iced tea.

Grace flashed a more sincere smile. "It's no big deal. My pleasure. And here you go, big brother." Grace handed him the glass and picked the tray back up. "Holler if you need anything else, I'm all yours until tomorrow morning."

"Why don't you join us?" Allison said.

"Nope. Aunt Eileen has us all in work mode. I swear that woman can think up more meaningless tasks than a Marine drill sergeant."

"And just like a DI, when Aunt Eileen says jump, no one asks how high," Ethan agreed.

Chuckling, Grace spun on her heel and returned to the kitchen mumbling, "Gotta love her."

Waving a finger after Grace, Allison asked softly, "Why until tomorrow?"

"She's going back to Dallas, she's got classes starting." Sitting up as much as he could with Brittany still sleeping on his chest, Ethan downed half the glass in one long, cool swallow.

Allison, on the other hand, took the tiniest sip and then leaned over to retrieve a small package from the bag. "I picked this up today from a little shop called Sisters. Are those two women really related?"

Ethan's chest rose and fell in time with his rumble of laughter. "Yeah, they really are sisters, and no we haven't any idea what their real names are."

"I see." She smiled and opened the lid on the box. "Do you think Brittany will like this?"

Putting the half-empty tea glass on the table beside him, he received the gift she'd held out to him. "Nice work." He turned it over and over again making the rattle sound. "She should love it."

"The sisters said it came from a local rancher, he only made one."

Local rancher. Ethan wondered.

"What?" Allison tipped her head, studying Ethan more closely. "Do you know who made it?"

"Maybe. One of the Brady brothers was always good with wood. I think we have a rocker he made. Took in payment for some cattle we sold him. Aunt Eileen treasures it."

"Why would a furniture maker whittle a baby rattle?"

"For his child."

Allison's eyes circled round. "Oh no."

"No. Nothing like that." Ethan knew where her mind had gone. "Around here folks get married and they've barely left the church when family and friends start asking for the babies. The Bradys all tend toward large families—"

"Like the Farradays?" There was a hint of humor in her tone.

"Yes." He smiled. "Like the Farradays. I think they were expecting to start popping them out but turned out his wife had some heart condition no one knew of. One morning she just didn't wake up."

"Oh my." Hand to her chest, she leaned back. "How sad is that."

"I'm only guessing that's who might have made the rattle. He had the Sisters sell some other pieces he'd made for their home."

"Well, it would certainly explain why he wanted a special baby to have it."

"Sisters said that?"

Allison nodded.

"Do you not want to give it to Brittany now?"

"No. I want her to have it. Sounds like it was made with a lot of love. She deserves that."

Ethan didn't need to be a genius who went to college at sixteen to read between the lines of what she hadn't said. The rattle was made with love, unlike Brittany. Well, he may not have loved Fancy, but he had more than enough love inside him already for his little girl and nothing in the world could be more important than that.

The buzzing sound of Allison's cell phone cut the silence in the room. Setting down the rattle, she reached into an outside pocket of her purse and, phone in hand, swiped at the screen. Her brows dipped into a confused V.

"What's wrong?" Ethan asked.

"Not wrong. Just odd. I don't recognize the number."

"What does it say?"

"Nothing important. Probably a wrong number."

• • • •

What the heck? *I made a terrible mistake.* Allison stared at the phone. Nothing else. A knot formed in the pit of her stomach. One possibility jumped to the forefront of her mind. Fancy. And Allison didn't like what that could mean one bit. She tapped out on the screen—*Who is this?*—and waited. Nothing. Maybe it was a wrong number. Maybe it wasn't Fancy. Maybe she had nothing to worry about. And maybe life was a bed of roses. "Well. Whoever it is will probably figure out their mistake."

"Won't be the first texting misconnect and I'm sure it won't be the last." Ethan shrugged.

Brittany stirred and Ethan dipped his chin to look at her. She wiggled again and Allison noticed both she and Ethan were fixated on Brittany as if she was the second coming. Two arms stretched out and eyes blinked open.

"She is a good baby."

"That's what everyone keeps telling me. I have nothing to compare her to. She's the first Farraday of her generation." Ethan kicked the recliner fully upright and shifted Brittany so she was resting on his arms rather than his chest. "Hi, Bree."

"Bree?"

"Finn started it and every once in a while I call her that too."

"One syllable sounds are easier for babies." Allison scooted forward. Waiting to see what Ethan was going to do next.

His gaze shifted from Brittany to her. "She's going to need a diaper change. Would you like the honors?"

He didn't have to ask twice. Allison sprang from her seat. In front of Ethan she extended her hands to her niece and was rewarded with a bright grin. Her own smile bloomed from a happy heart.

"Everything you need is by the porta-crib." He pointed to the set-up on his other side.

Bending over for the occasional tummy nuzzle or finger tickle, Allison made quick work of changing the diaper.

When she straightened with Brittany on her hip, Ethan was smiling at her. "You've had practice."

"Yeah, you could say that." Though he was watching her and the baby, Allison noticed he was running his thumb across his fingers on his injured hand again. "Something wrong?"

He glanced down at the hand as though just noticing what he'd been doing. "Oh, no. Just feels funny not being all bandaged."

Without saying a word, she returned Brittany to the porta-crib and pulled Ethan's hand toward her. Running her fingers along the edge of his palm, she scanned the hand from tip to base, pressed her thumb here and there checking for white spots and blood flow. The scar ran the length of his palm. She pinched a fingertip. "You had quite a lot of stitches. Pretty deep laceration. I'm amazed you've been able to get around so well on the crutches."

Ethan shrugged. "Until that first day in the park I'd been forced to use a wheelchair. Hated it."

"I bet you did."

"Keeping my movement to a minimum and the bulky bandaging helped."

Allison nodded, pinched another finger and glanced up at him then back. She repeated it from finger to finger. "Close your fist for me."

He did as he was told. All the light had gone from his eyes. Ethan the Marine was in front of her now.

"Are you doing any therapy for it?" She closed her hand over his and watched his face.

"I've been doing some exercises the doctor gave me."

She nodded at him. "How's the feeling?"

For a moment something akin to surprise, or maybe fear, flashed in his eyes and then disappeared behind the guarded Marine façade. "Fine." Reaching for his crutches, he blew out a heavy breath, then pushed to his feet and settled in front of Brittany, his happy father smile back in place. "It's almost supper time. We should probably check what's happening in the kitchen. Would you mind carrying Brittany for me?"

"Not at all." Ethan had no idea how lucky he was to be blessed with a baby with such a pleasant disposition. Brittany probably didn't have colic or any other attitude challenging issues. Infant snuggled in her arms, she watched Ethan swing his way across the room. The man did have one hell of a physique. And if she wasn't mistaken, a secret. When she returned to her laptop tonight she was going to have to add something new to her to-do list.

• • • •

Ethan made his way into the kitchen, Allison and Brittany on his heels. Eileen wasn't sure what the heck was going on in the other room, but from her limited view of the hand holding, sparks of some kind or other should start flying any time now. And the way she saw it, sooner would be better than later.

"All right. Everyone grab a dish and head for the dining room." She turned to Allison. "Not you dear. You've got precious cargo. There's a swing by Ethan's seat. If you want, you can set her in there."

"If you don't mind I'd like to hold her a little longer."

"Don't mind at all." Eileen patted her arm.

From the back door, Finn headed straight for Allison and the baby. Eileen grabbed the bowl of mashed potatoes and before Finn could get within two feet, shoved them at him. "Put these on the table, please."

Smiling at his niece, he nodded at his aunt. "Yes, ma'am."

"Ethan," Eileen looked to her nephew standing beside his daughter. "Let Allison have your seat near the swing. You can sit to her right."

For a split second Eileen thought her nephew was going to object. Instead, like his younger brother, he nodded. "Yes, ma'am."

All of her family gathering around the table, the boys pulling out the chairs for the women, happy faces, food moving back and forth, and Ethan balancing on his crutches and helping Allison, she had to smile. Some days things just had a way of going nothing but right.

CHAPTER FIFTEEN

Holding the ice cold water glass with his recovering hand, Ethan willed his three middle fingers to feel something. Allison hadn't said anything, but he was sure she knew. With every touch and poke, he ignored the electricity zinging up his arm. She was his daughter's aunt. The sister of the woman who'd given life to his baby. He was not supposed to be attracted to her.

Only her pointed questions about his hand had squelched the feelings pinging around inside him like a cool bucket of ice water. The hand specialist had done well. He had full use of all his fingers. Even in his drug-induced haze those first days in the hospital, he'd seen the concern in the man's eyes as he'd examined the sutured flesh followed by the relief as Ethan moved each finger one by one.

With every bandage change since Ethan's arrival home, Brooks had shown his pleasure with Ethan's dexterity. Not until Brooks explained the risks of nerve damage with his type of wound did Ethan understand the original concern in his doctor's eyes. Now he felt a new concern. A numbness in his fingertips that didn't want to clear up.

"This was delicious." Allison pointed at the green bean casserole with her fork before setting it down beside the knife on her empty plate. "Seriously amazing. I normally don't care for green beans."

"Thank you," Aunt Eileen beamed. "It was definitely a group effort."

"I'll say," Meg agreed. "I'm not usually allowed to help in the kitchen. Of course the fact that I'm not the best cook might have something to do with that."

"Nope," Toni shook her head, "I'm not usually allowed to help either."

"And she can cook," Brooks waved a thumb at his wife, then leaned over and kissed the tip of her nose, making her smile.

"Just goes to show," Finn looked to his aunt, "it takes an entire family to do what you do every Sunday. But," he raised a single finger, "the next time a vacation opportunity comes along with the social club you have no excuse to refuse. It may take an army of Farradays to pull it off, but we won't starve."

Aunt Eileen shrugged off the comment and Ethan noticed his father eyeing his aunt, not with the usual appreciation that he showed to the woman who had come in and saved his family, but intently, as though he were searching for the first parts of a thousand-piece puzzle.

Either unaware, or perhaps merely ignoring the way her brother-in-law studied her, Aunt Eileen pushed away from the table. "If we want the dessert Toni brought, we'd better get the table cleared off."

"What dessert might that be?" Adam stood and picked up his plate and the bowl of mashed potatoes.

"German chocolate cake." Toni smiled.

"Oh," Meg groaned. "I can feel my waist expanding already."

Aunt Eileen reached for the breadbasket only to have DJ sidle up beside her. "I'll take that. Cook shouldn't clean up."

"I'll take yours," Allison stood and reached for Ethan's dish.

"No, no." Aunt Eileen shook her head. "Guests don't clear either."

DJ, who'd sat beside her, smiled and took the dish from her hand. "Aunt Eileen is right. House rules."

"So," Aunt Eileen leaned forward, "do you know any more about how long you'll be staying?"

Allison cast a quick peek at the baby now in her father's arms. "No, I don't."

"Well." Clasping her hands together almost in prayer, Aunt Eileen smiled. "If the goal is to spend time with your niece then I think you should come stay with us."

Allison's eyes bugged open wide and Ethan was pretty sure his had just done the same. Only DJ and Becky were close enough to have heard and even they did a double take.

"Oh, that's very generous of you, but—"

"Nothing generous about it at all. We have plenty of room and with this brood one more mouth to feed is nothing."

"Well, thank you, but—"

"Besides, if we put you into the room across the hall from Ethan we can move Brittany downstairs with her father."

"Oh, yes, but—"

"Ethan still can't do late night feedings with those crutches."

"No, I can see where he couldn't."

Aunt Eileen stood. "Frankly, I could use a good night's sleep, and you wouldn't mind helping out with that would you?"

"Uhm, if I were here of course not, but—"

"Good, then it's settled." With a nod Aunt Eileen stepped away from the table and called to the kitchen. "Sean, you or one of the boys will need to bring the baby carriage downstairs."

Ethan managed to snap his mouth shut. Allison on the other hand, stared at him with her mouth still open, her objections unspoken and futile.

Hurricane Eileen had struck.

• • • •

The room across the hall from where Ethan slept was barely large enough for a full bed with a small nightstand on either side. If she'd eaten any more dessert Allison would have to walk sideways to climb into bed.

Between supper and dessert, voices lowered, the Farraday patriarch and his sister-in-law had shared words in the kitchen, but whether it was about Allison staying or the weather, she didn't have a clue. The chocolate cake was served, conversation carried on around her, and Allison couldn't figure out how she'd so easily let herself get roped into a situation that could not end well. Nor for the life of her could she figure a polite way out of it either.

With everyone clearing the table and moving about with miscellaneous chores, Aunt Eileen had shown Allison the extra room and left her standing in the hall to get clean towels.

"You don't have to go through with this." Ethan had come up behind her.

Still stunned at the turn of events, Allison was at a loss for words.

"Are you okay? I just heard what happened?" Meg squeezed past Ethan and came up to Allison. "She did the same thing to me when I first arrived. There really is no point in fighting it. That woman is the personification of a force to be reckoned with."

"Hey man." Finn stopped in the doorway beside his brother and gently slapped his shoulder. "I'm sorry, I thought we'd talked her out of it. I can give it another shot if you want."

Ethan looked to Allison. The decision was hers, she wasn't sure how she knew that's what his eyes said, but she *was* sure of the message. "I don't know what to say."

"It's that damn dog." Finn shook his head.

"Our dog?" Meg asked.

Ethan's brow scrunched in confusion. "When did you get a dog?"

"She doesn't mean her dog," Finn chimed in, "she means the dog that has been popping up—"

"And disappearing," Meg added.

"And disappearing," Finn agreed, "for her and Adam, Brooks and Toni, Connor and Catherine, DJ and Becky—"

"I think I see a pattern here," Allison mumbled.

Ethan rubbed two fingers against his temple.

"Yeah," Finn nodded at his brother. "I know."

Meg waved a hand from Ethan to Allison. "I don't see what our dog has to do with them."

"We were introduced the first time by a dog," Allison said in a near whisper.

"In California," Ethan added.

Meg lifted her hands to her waist. "Well then, that can't be our dog."

DJ appeared behind Ethan and Finn. "Are we having a party and not inviting the rest of the family?"

"We're discussing the dog." Meg said. "*The* dog."

"In California," Ethan enunciated carefully.

"And Tuckers Bluff," DJ added.

Meg and Finn turned to DJ in surprise and DJ spread his arms wide apart, palms up. "Hey, it's not my fault Cupid decided to show up at the café while Papa and Auntie ate lunch at separate tables."

"That dog?" Another piece of the puzzle fell into place for Allison. "The one watching us from the curb?"

DJ nodded, Finn smiled, Meg shook her head, and Ethan sighed.

"If it's not this," Allison looked to Ethan, "it's going to be something else, isn't it?"

All four Farraday heads nodded.

"Well," she pushed her sleeves up her arms and lifted her chin, "which one of you is going with me to town to get my things as your aunt suggested?"

"You're staying?" Ethan's voice almost cracked with surprise.

"The way I see it, there's only one way to convince your aunt that mutt in San Diego—or the parking lot—isn't playing Cupid. We've got to prove her wrong."

"I'd better go," Finn volunteered. "Gimpy here won't be much help with the luggage or the driving."

Ethan shot his brother a say-that-again-in-a-month glare. Finn merely shrugged a lazy shoulder and flashed a sly grin in response. Allison had the feeling that despite being the youngest son, Finn ruled the roost more often than not. She also hoped that when all was said and done, agreeing to this scheme didn't make her crazier than Aunt Eileen.

• • • •

His aunt was totally out of her damn mind. For the two hours that Finn and Allison were gone to town and back, Ethan and his dad had done their best to convince Aunt Eileen to keep Brittany upstairs with her, but she'd have none of it. Not even when Ethan had shared the fear he might wake up with one of his nightmares and disturb, or heaven forbid, hurt Brittany, did his aunt acquiesce. Instead, she'd merely pointed out that every night since his arrival at the ranch he'd slept till morning like the proverbial baby. Now every time Brittany let out the slightest peep, he'd stick out his hand and rock the baby carriage.

The clock on his nightstand blinked 2:30 a.m. He and his daughter had gone to bed at about the same time and Ethan didn't think he'd gotten a lick of sleep waiting for her to wake up. Another fifteen minutes went by and another peep and another rock-a-bye-baby. Another fifteen minutes and another repeat. By 3:15 Brittany was awake and very vocal.

"There, there, sweetie." He spun around and sat on the edge of the bed. His hand on her tummy seemed to sooth her some.

"I'll get the bottle."

By the time he'd turned to the voice, Allison was gone. Using the nightstand for leverage, he shoved to his feet and, balancing on one foot, peered into the buggy. "Bet you're surprised to see me, aren't you?"

Instead of the usual bright grin, Brittany offered her father a curious stare.

At least changing diapers had become less of a challenge without the massive bandage. Able to grab hold of her legs with his recovering hand, his good hand had the fine motor skills to peel off the old diaper and hold on to the fresh one.

"How's it going?" Allison appeared at his side.

"All dry and ready for her snack." Ethan handed Brittany over to her aunt.

Despite the late hour, Allison smiled sweetly down at the

baby in her arm. "Just remember when you're all grown up, snacking in the middle of the night is a terrible idea."

Brittany didn't have a smile for her aunt either. The poor kid seemed to be thoroughly confused by the change in nighttime shift. At least she wasn't squalling for his aunt. When Allison teased her lips with the tip of the bottle, Brittany caught on to the new plan and her cheeks pumped with gusto, her gaze never leaving Allison's face.

"Now I understand that mother rock." Her hips swaying from side to side, Allison shifted her attention from the baby to Ethan before looking around the room.

"Why don't you have a—" For as long as he could remember there had always been a chair in the corner of this room. More than once he'd tossed his clothes onto the checkered easy chair. Now it was gone. His aunt. He held back a sigh. "There's a rocker in the den if you want to sit down with her."

Allison shook her head, but after another minute or so, she glanced downward at his bed. "Do you mind?"

"No. Of course not."

Stepping aside, she sat on the very edge, her back to him. She continued to sway in place and in no time the bottle was empty and Allison was back on her feet, pacing with Brittany. "She's a really good eater."

He nodded and his daughter let out a belch to echo her agreement. A few more sways and the baby was sound asleep once again. He continued to watch as Allison made her way around to the other side of the buggy and gently lowered his daughter onto the mattress.

Allison straightened. "That went well."

Ethan nodded. Better than he'd expected. "We'd should get some sleep before the six o'clock feeding."

"Night."

"Goodnight." Ethan did a quick survey of his daughter before sliding under the covers. Tomorrow he was going to have a long talk with his aunt.

CHAPTER SIXTEEN

A nother poker chip landed in the pile. So excited by the turn of events, Eileen called for a weekend game at the café.

"I can't believe you pulled it off." Ruth Ann showed her hand. "A pair of ladies over tens."

"It was actually much easier than I'd thought." Eileen tossed her cards to Sally May. "Turns out Meg is way better at mashing potatoes than she lets on, Adam and Brooks will stay in any room their wives are in, and somehow keeping Allison and Ethan alone in the big room just came together."

Sally May shuffled the cards. "And no one said anything when you cleaned up the storage room?"

"No. That was a brilliant suggestion." Eileen cut the deck. "Thankfully that old full bed was already against the wall so I didn't have to get help lugging a bed down from upstairs. Only took a couple of hours after the men went to bed to move half the boxes up to the attic and toss stuff we had no business storing into the trash. Then took another hour in the morning to clean and straighten up and no one noticed. Element of surprise with the room all ready for guests was on my side."

"Surprise is one word for it," Dorothy said.

Sally May dealt out the first round of cards. "Bet ambush was more like it."

Eileen had to laugh with her friends of so many years. They knew her too well. It *had* been rather like a military maneuver. "Having Allison staying in the same house was one thing, but across the hall by themselves should work like a charm. This morning, I pretended to sleep in, but sneaked by the kitchen a minute to eavesdrop on the morning feeding."

"And?" Dorothy asked.

"Simple talk. Pass me this, hand me that. Do you want to feed her this time? Teamwork has begun. It was as if they'd been working together for way more than one night."

"I suppose," Ruth Ann held her hand out waiting for the next card, "I may have been overly skeptical. But I seriously couldn't see Sean going along with this idea of throwing these two together."

"Why not?" Eileen picked up her last card. "It's in everyone's best interest for Ethan and Allison to make nice and not fight over Brittany. Even if Allison doesn't have a legal leg to stand on, her and Ethan on opposite sides of a tug of war won't be good for the baby."

"Has she said that's what she wants?" Dorothy asked.

"No. But why else would she be here?"

"True." Dorothy fanned out her cards. "On both counts."

"And that's exactly why last night in the kitchen Sean had to finally agree with me." Eileen smiled at her cards. Three queens. "Sometimes difficult situations take extreme measures."

"Okay." Ruth Ann pulled out two cards from her hand and set them face down beside her. "So you've conned the unsuspecting woman into your lair. You've maneuvered the two targets into close quarters. What's next on the plan, oh mastermind?"

"Simple." Eileen tossed two chips into the pot and smiled at her friends. "I think I feel a bad case of the flu coming on."

● ● ● ●

"Yes, Mark, I understand." Phone in her hand, Allison paced on the Farraday back porch as she spoke to her boss. "I don't know how much longer I'll be." What she had hoped to find out here in Texas was a frazzled single man anxious to get back to his job and happy to turn over a baby to her aunt.

"All right." Mark sighed. "I know you've been questioning the direction your career has taken, but that's not what this is about. Are you going to tell me what's really going on?"

"It's complicated."

"Only if you make it so. When you flew out of here like an avenging angel, the only thing you cared about was that your niece was well taken care of."

"I know. And that's still true." She hadn't dared tell her boss that she'd been planning to become a single aunt and debate with him the problems that came with that and being a surgeon at a busy metropolitan hospital.

"Is she well cared for?"

"Yes."

"Wanting for anything?"

Allison sighed. "No."

"But you're still there?"

"Yes. It's—"

"Complicated. Yeah, I got that. Look, you don't need me to tell you how long and hard you worked to be one of the most respected physicians in the state of California."

"Only California?" She smiled.

"My point, Dr. Monroe, is I'll tell the board whatever you want me to, but make sure you know what you really want and don't throw away everything you've worked for out of guilt over your sister."

"Thank you Dr. Freud."

Mark chuckled, his voice lowered an octave. "We're all worried about you." He paused. "I'm worried about you."

Allison stopped walking and looked to the expanse of land nestled under a clear blue sky as far as her eyes could see. "I'll let you know when I'll be coming home."

"All right. And Allison…"

"Yes?"

"Be careful." The call disconnected before she could respond. How did he always know when she was in over her head? Weren't women supposed to be the one with stellar intuition?

The screen door squeaked and Ethan stepped onto the porch.

"Once again Mistress Brittany is sleeping soundly. I'd offer you something cool to drink, but…" Leaning on the crutches he moved his hands to point to the metallic appendages.

"You're getting pretty tired of them, aren't you?" She slipped her phone into her pocket and leaned back on the railing.

"Oh yeah. I was tired of this leg the moment the meds wore off." He crossed the width of the porch and placing the crutches to one side, settled onto the railing a few feet beside her. "If it weren't for Brittany, I'd be as antsy as a caged lion."

"She can't possibly keep you that busy."

"More like entertained." His attention drifted to the large kitchen window, and his expression darkened.

"What's got you so worried?" she asked.

He turned to face her. "Who says I'm worried?"

"Okay, you're not worried." She crossed her arms. "Penny for your thoughts?"

Looking down, his thumb brushed against his middle fingers. "Did you know that a pilot does not have to have feeling in his middle fingers to operate a helicopter?"

"Only general mobility and range of motion."

"That's right." He looked at her with surprise.

A smile tugged at her lips. "I looked it up."

Nodding, he continued to look at his hand for another few beats then raised his eyes to meet hers. "Did you also look up that numbness or nerve damage to fingers will ground a pilot in the military?"

The other night, when she'd checked his hand she'd suspected something like this. "Yes."

"Growing up, whenever we didn't get something we wanted, Aunt Eileen was fond of reminding us when a door closes look for an open window." He turned to the kitchen window. "Right now the only thing stopping me from losing my mind is that thirteen pound bundle of gurgling smiles on the other side of that wall."

Allison pushed away from the railing and stepped in front of Ethan. "Let me see the hand."

For a second, she thought he was going to refuse. Then, palm up, he held his hand out for her to examine. She poked, and tapped, much like she had the night before. She retrieved her phone, removed the built-in stylus, put the phone back and began tapping at his hand. "Do you feel this?"

He nodded.

She tapped some more. "What about here?"

"Yeah."

Slowly she worked her way across different portions of his hand until the response changed to "I feel pressure but not the stick."

By the time she reached the base of his fingers the feeling was almost completely gone.

"Well. What's your official report?"

Still holding onto the hand she shook her head. "There are a lot of factors. Once repair is made the damage begins to heal in three to four weeks."

"It's been that," he said softly.

"Yes. But," she touched the numbed flesh, "this area of damage could take as long as a year to fully heal and restore sensation."

"A year," he repeated under his breath.

"There's still hope." She wanted very much for there to be more than hope. The pain reflected in his eyes shot through her like a shard of shattered glass. The intensity caught her completely by surprise. The shock of it had her dropping his hand as though it too were broken glass. "I, uh, should check on Brittany, or maybe see what I can do to help before your aunt comes home. Or … something."

"Yeah," his throat tightened with a long swallow. "Something."

For whatever reason her feet seemed rooted to the ground. She'd managed a short step back as he reached for the crutches. When he'd pushed to a standing position he was only inches away from her. Clear green eyes flashed bright and then instantly darkened. Muscles along his jaw line corded with tension. Her mind shouted *move* but her feet remained planted in cement. The need to stretch onto her tippy toes and taste lips now thinly pressed together was so strong she could barely catch her breath. She felt herself rock on her heels and heard the smack of an aluminum crutch on wooden floor at the same second a strong arm slid around her waist and moist lips covered hers.

Sanity should have had her pulling away, but the press of his hand at the small of her back and the tender touch of his lips gently tasting hers made her never want to run away again.

"Allison," her name rode the warm breath that caressed her mouth. Ethan's hand eased slowly away. His weight shifted, finding balance without her. "I shouldn't have done that."

Sucking in a fortifying breath, she took a step in retreat, almost tripping over herself, stumbling out of the way.

Strong fingers curled around her arm. "Careful." Ethan spoke so low she could barely hear him.

"Yes."

"I'm sorry."

Nodding, she turned and had to force herself to take slow measured steps combating the impulse to run inside. She'd made it all the way to her room, closed the door and, back pressed to the wall, blew out the air trapped in her lungs. What the hell was she doing?

• • • •

Ethan wished to hell he hadn't come out onto the porch. Then the feel of her skin under his fingers, her warmth pressed against him, wouldn't be seared in his mind. Last night when she'd held his hand, he'd had to focus on the medical nature of her ministrations. He'd done the same thing a few minutes ago in anticipation of her touch, but when he'd stood and found himself so close, so very close, and she didn't move, there had been no mental preparation. And no restraint. One minute he was gathering all the self restraint he could muster and the next thing he knew he had her in his arms and freely taking what she wasn't offering. He'd made a mistake. He was supposed to keep an eye on her, not his hands. Or his mouth. And damned if he didn't want to go back inside and pull her into his arms again, and this time not stop.

Served him right for not minding his own business. With the kitchen window open he could hear the conversation meant to be private. When her phone rang she'd stepped outside and placed the call on speaker, not realizing Ethan could hear every word. If he'd been a better man he would have returned to the living room and given Allison the privacy she wanted, but something stronger than the decent streak he'd been raised with had him hanging on every word. At first the conversation sounded like any communication between people who worked together and he'd listened for some additional information of her intentions. Then the conversation took on a personal tone that left Ethan wondering who this was. A boss, a friend, a lover? Not that it was any of his business, but he'd also detected a sadness in her voice that against his better judgment had him following her outside and planting himself way too close. Or had the question nagging at the back of his mind over the mystery man on the phone been what prompted Ethan to find out for himself if she belonged to another man.

Either way, now he had no idea who she'd been speaking to, but the way she melted against him, the guy on the line was definitely not her lover, and Ethan hadn't a clue as to why she'd sounded so disheartened on the phone. What he did know was the taste and feel of her, both dangerous pieces of knowledge.

Crutches in place, he wished he had two good legs to detour to the barn. Every one of his siblings had a different love. His had been things that went really fast and really high. But when something ate at the heart or soul, it was the barn, the hard work, and the horses that got the Farradays through. He desperately needed the distraction of hard work.

The screen door slammed shut behind him and he crossed through the kitchen into the den. Careful not to look at Allison, he dropped into the recliner. On the loveseat across from him, brows furrowed, Allison tapped away at her computer. In her porta-crib beside him, Brittany slept so peacefully. If only he could bottle that peace of mind. Just as he was reaching for the remote control, the chime of a text message on his phone rang out. Allison's gaze lifted from the keyboard. Their eyes met, and her cheeks filled with that familiar hue of pink.

Everything about his world had gone totally crazy. A few swipes and an unknown number appeared with the message: *I've changed my mind.*

Bashfulness hid behind Allison's concerned eyes. "You're frowning."

"Just got the strangest text. Whoever it is has changed their mind about something." When he looked back at Allison from the phone, all color had drained from her face.

Practically tossing the computer aside, she sprang off the couch, ran from the room and reappeared with her cell in hand. "What's the number?"

"Area code 251—"

"941," she filled in.

"Yeah. 5555."

"Oh, God," Allison sank into the nearest seat.

"What am I missing?" he asked, too tired to think for himself.

"Remember my strange text the other day?"

He had to think a minute. "The wrong number?"

Allison nodded. Shaking hands passed him her phone.

"*I've made a terrible mistake,*" he read softly, then lifted his gaze to meet hers. He couldn't voice the possibility that popped into his head.

Wringing her fingers, she sucked in a deep breath. "It occurred to me it might be Fancy, but when she didn't respond, I convinced myself it really was a mistake."

"Where the hell is the 251 area code?" Ethan swiped at his screen and plugged in the numbers in question. "Alabama Gulf Coast."

"Alabama?"

If they were right and the caller was Fancy, he had no idea why she was in Alabama, but as far as he was concerned, Antarctica wasn't far enough away. "I'd better call DJ."

Allison nodded, reached out, and grabbed his wrist. "If it's her…"

He bobbed his head.

"If Fancy's changed her mind… We can't let her have Brittany…The things the detective told me." She shook her head and took a deep breath. "I don't want to imagine the life that sweet baby would have if she were left and forgotten in some seedy apartment with who knows who."

He nodded at her. Even if all evidence showed Fancy had done a good job with Brittany for the first two months of her life, and bringing her to him also showed some common sense on Fancy's part, he still didn't want to even consider Allison's nightmare scenario, never mind repeat it out loud.

"Promise me?" She squeezed his wrist.

"Trust me. Come hell or high water, no one is taking my daughter. If it comes down to my cold dead body, there are six more Farradays who will make sure that little girl stays right where she belongs."

Allison sucked in a deep shaky breath and Ethan had the feeling he'd just confirmed her worst fears. What she'd come all the way to Texas to uncover. If it was Brittany Allison wanted, she and her sister were just shit out of luck.

CHAPTER SEVENTEEN

The family police chief had little to say about the texts but agreed to look into it. Until the rest of the family came home, Allison buried her nose in her laptop and Ethan played with Brittany. Allison had desperately wanted to join in on the odd efforts at Patty Cake and This Little Piggy, but she didn't dare get close to Ethan, so like a coward, she did nothing.

Her reprieve came with the arrival of the working Farradays.

From the kitchen Finn headed straight to Brittany. "Hey there, sweet thing. Uncle Finn is home." He pulled her up in the air and held her high over his head, making her giggle. Next, he pulled her down against his face, blew into her tummy, and Brittany would laugh even harder. After several minutes of that, he settled her in one arm and looked around the room. "Don't y'all look nice and domestic. Opposite sides of the room like old married people."

The statement should have made her laugh. It was a joke. Said in fun. But panic coursed through her at the ludicrous fear that somehow Finn knew they'd been kissing. Had he been near the house? Had he seen them? Was it written all over her face? Geeky doctor got kissed by hunky cowboy? Oh Lord, it was all she could do not to hyperventilate.

The front door opened and Aunt Eileen walked in. She too headed straight for Brittany and practically snatched the baby from her uncle's arms. "Boy did I miss you today."

Allison dared a glance in Ethan's direction and noticed his stiff posture. Had the harmless comment from his brother affected Ethan the same way it had her? So what? So they kissed. People did it all the time. She really needed to get a grip.

"Sean should be coming in shortly. I'd better get supper warmed and on the table."

"I'll help." Allison jumped to her feet. Anything to keep her mind off kissing and Ethan.

"Works for me." Aunt Eileen handed the baby back to her father and turned for the kitchen. "You have a good day?"

"Yeah, yes."

Aunt Eileen pulled a huge foil covered tray from the fridge. "Why don't you grab some fixings for salad. These boys like their meat and potatoes but I gotta get some greens in them too."

"Sure." Glad to have something to do with her hands, she pulled lettuce and a few *fixings,* as Aunt Eileen had said, from the vegetable bin and began dicing.

Aunt Eileen closed the oven door and fiddled with the knobs. When she looked at Allison her brows crinkled together. "You sure you had a good day? Baby didn't give you any trouble, did she?"

"No. Brittany was fine. I just…" She wasn't going to say got rattled by the best kiss she'd ever had. Not that she'd had that many to compare it to. "Had a few work things to deal with. Spoke with the head of my department today."

Aunt Eileen opened the bread bin and pulled out a loaf of unsliced bread along with a large knife. "Nothing serious I hope?"

"No, no. But you know how it is."

"Did you know," Ethan's aunt paused from cutting thick slices and waved the long serrated knife in the air, "that Brooks is opening a small clinic?"

"Really?" She tossed the pepper into a bowl and reached for a tomato. "I wouldn't think there's that much need out here."

"Nearest hospital is ninety miles away and for the serious stuff folks have to go all the way to Abilene or Lubbock."

"Yes. I could see why."

"Some trauma cases have been airlifted all the way to Dallas."

"Yes, well. I'm not surprised." She continued dicing.

Aunt Eileen slathered butter on the one-inch-thick slices of bread. "When folks closer to Tuckers Bluff start coming here instead of trucking all the way to Butler Springs, Brooks isn't going to be able to handle the load on his own."

Allison raised a brow at the woman.

"Of course country doctorin' isn't like a big city hospital."

"No," Allison smiled. "I'm sure it's not." But at least it's a far cry better than a tent in the jungle. "Are there a lot of folks around here who can't afford medical care?"

Eileen scoffed, "Not everyone around these parts has a spread like this. We've got all kinds of folks eking a living from the land, and most have big families. The days of doctors getting paid with chickens and eggs are gone for the most part, but sometimes..." She let her words hang.

Allison got the message.

"That smells great." Sean came in the back door, hung his hat on a nearby hook and went straight to the sink to wash his hands. Allison felt like a character in an old western TV show. All she needed was the apron and a dog.

The rest of the evening went more or less the same way. She and Ethan avoided getting within ten feet of each other, the family laughed, and chatted, and teased all through dinner, and Brittany was pretty much the light of the room and center of attention all the way to bedtime.

Thirty minutes into a re-run of Sean Farraday's favorite TV show, Aunt Eileen stood, a cup of warm tea in her hand, and yawned. "I think I'm going to call it a night early. Feeling a bit tired."

Sean nodded, Finn had gone off to his room right after supper and Ethan winked. The roguish gesture made his aunt laugh and in turn Allison saw the first sincere smile of the day on Ethan's face. She was thinking now would be as good time as any to make her escape when Ethan's phone rang and his lips tightened.

"Yeah." Looking to Allison, Ethan mouthed, "DJ."

She inched to the edge of the sofa, not able to hear a blessed thing other than Ethan's occasional grunt.

"All right. I'll check with my lawyer. See if we can't hurry up that blasted appearance before the judge. And thanks, bro." Ethan set his phone aside.

"Well, is it her?"

"The number is a throw away phone bought at a convenience store in Mobile. A friend of DJ's had someone go flash Francine's driver's license photo. It was her. Apparently she's not alone. Traveling with a man. They'd spent a couple of nights in a fleabag motel and then moved on. That's all he knows for now."

Sean Farraday had lowered the volume on the TV as soon as Ethan began speaking. "What is this all about?"

Ethan sighed. "Both Allison and I received cryptic texts from the same number. The only thing we have in common is her sister."

Her sister. Not Brittany's mother. Not even his ex, but her sister. What did that tell about how this entire crazy situation was evolving?

Ethan's father shook his head. "Whatever is going on with that poor woman, DJ will be on top of it, but we need to get things official once and for all." He turned off the TV. "I think I've had enough of the world for one night. Don't stay up too late."

"No, sir," Ethan responded.

"Goodnight." His father waved at the two of them and made his way up the stairs.

"He's right." Ethan pushed to his feet. "I'm going to see if I can't get some sleep."

Allison nodded and turned. Maybe sleep would make sense of everything.

Only it didn't help a blessed thing. For hours Allison tossed and turned. If she wasn't worrying about Fancy she was anxiously anticipating Brittany waking up and having to work with Ethan in his small room. Though it wasn't so much the size of the room that was a problem for her but the size of the large bed in the middle. Yesterday the bed hadn't made any impact on her. Tonight, after that unexpected kiss, the bed seemed to jump to the forefront of her mind.

According to the clock at her bedside table Brittany's complaints came across the narrow hall into Allison's room right on time at a little after three. Throwing back the blankets, she sucked in a deep breath and wiped at her eyes. She'd faced down two- and four-legged leeches, so one good looking cowboy wasn't going to get the best of her. At least that's what she'd been reminding herself for hours. Even though she'd gone to bed in sleeping pants and a t-shirt, she took a minute to throw on her bathrobe. At Ethan's door, without actually stopping, she called to him, "I'll get the bottle," and went straight for the kitchen.

When she came back to the room, Ethan secured the last tape tab on the diaper and lifted Brittany into his arms. Poor guy looked as tired as Allison felt. And she might be oversensitive, but she was pretty sure he was avoiding looking her in the eye.

"Do you want me to feed her or are you up to it?"

"I can do it." With his daughter in the crook of his arm, he accepted the bottle.

Allison waited a few moments. "When you're done put the bottle on the night table. I'm going back to bed. Guess I'll see you in the morning."

Lifting his gaze to meet hers, Ethan flashed a very tired smile. "Why don't you sit down a minute. I think we should talk."

"Now?" They'd had all evening to talk and he'd hardly said two words to her after speaking to his brother.

"Now is about the only time it will be just the two of us."

He was right about that. "Okay," she took a seat on the edge of the bed. "What's on your mind?"

• • • •

That was something Allison did not want to know. Even if Ethan knew that what was on his mind would make those cheeks of hers flush a pretty shade of pink. "What are your intentions?"

"My intentions?"

"As soon as the judge signs off on the release of parental rights, Brittany's future with me will be secure. If Fancy has indeed changed her mind and wants Brittany back before the judge signs off on it, that could be a mess." Allison nodded and Ethan went over the words that he'd rehearsed for hours. "You said before we can't let that happen."

"I did."

"Because you'll stand by me or because you want Brittany yourself?"

Allison's eyes opened wide and for a second he thought she might sway off the edge of the bed. Her eyes shifted to Brittany sucking at her bottle, and then, squeezing those same eyes shut, Allison blew out a soft sigh and lifted her lids to level her gaze with his. "When I first heard about Brittany I thought there had to be some mistake. That there was another Francine Monroe Langdon out there. Once I was convinced Brittany was indeed my niece, my only thought was getting to her. I was going to make damn sure she had a better childhood than either me or Francine and I sure as hell wasn't going to let her turn out like her mother."

He could see why she might feel that way. Even though Fancy had a good heart, she had plenty of bad habits. Most he hadn't seen for himself, but in their brief time together Fancy had almost used him as a therapist. They'd actually spent more time talking, or in his case listening, than they had *other* things.

"I knew your family seemed like nice people on the surface. But you're a man. What do you know about raising a little girl?"

He heard himself chuckle, and at the flare of annoyance in her eyes, he spoke up quickly. "Don't think I haven't asked myself that same question a hundred times."

"See." Her shoulders relaxed and she scooted further in on the bed. "I'd convinced myself, even if you turned out to be a better man than a weekend hookup would imply—"

"Ouch." Away from Tuckers Bluff a woman in every port seemed perfectly normal, but the way Allison spat the word *hookup* made him feel like pond scum.

She rolled her eyes. "Face it, the world is filled with a lot more fathers who just walked away than mothers."

"I don't think this is the time to go there."

"No." Her gaze settled on Brittany and softened. "But you can't blame me for thinking a swashbuckling jet jock—"

"Those are fighter pilots."

"And you don't fight?" She straightened her spine. "I suppose you broke that ankle bowling."

This was no time to quibble over semantics or nicknames. He shook his head.

"I rest my case." Her shoulders relaxed again. "It wasn't out of line for me to think as a man whose visits home on leave are few and far between that you might be relieved to have someone take a baby off your hands."

"Is that what you thought would happen? That you'd find a frazzled single dad who knew more about lift and drag than diapers and burping?"

Slowly her head bobbed.

The bottle empty, he set it aside and shifted Brittany to his shoulder, patted her back. "As you can see I've mastered burping."

A sweet smile crossed Allison's lips and his conscience kicked his ego to the curb.

"If I didn't have the help of my family I probably would have been exactly what you expected," he raised a silencing finger at her when she started to speak, "but, I still would have found a way to make this work." The fact that he was still figuring all of that out in his own mind was irrelevant. And as he was starting to realize, going back to fly for Uncle Sam might not be the obstacle he feared.

Allison drew in a deep breath and let out a long heavy sigh. "Which is why, as hard as it is, I do believe you and your family can provide Brittany with a better life than I can."

He had to think about that a second. He knew Allison made an excellent living, or perhaps she might be low on funds at the moment from running around the world, but a successful surgeon should be able to provide for her niece and yet …

"After all," a smile bloomed out of her sad expression, "what little girl wouldn't want to grow up with a real pony?"

"Thank you." Brittany had long ago burped and fallen asleep, but he held on to her anyhow like a much-needed security blanket.

Palms flat on her thighs, Allison nodded and pushed herself upright. "And with that finally established, I have a boss anxious to get me home and back in the operating room, so it's probably best I pack up and head to the airport tomorrow."

Ethan nodded. What more could he say?

"If I hear any more from my sister I'll let you know, and if you need me to help with the judge..."

"Thanks."

She nodded, the smile faded, and he watched her back as she crossed the hall. She was right. It was time for her to get back to her life and for him and Brittany to move on with theirs. So why did he feel like he'd just been kicked in the teeth?

CHAPTER EIGHTEEN

Doors slamming, pans banging, and male voices mumbling snapped Allison out of a deep sleep. As much as giving up her claim to Brittany hurt, an unexpected sense of calm washed over her as soon as she'd made the choice. Another pot clanked followed by a colorful four letter word and Allison decided she'd better see what the heck was going on.

Sean Farraday stood by the stove, a cooking fork in one hand and the pointer finger of his other in his mouth. Ethan had Brittany on one shoulder while he scooped beans into the coffee maker, and Finn looked up from all fours, paper towels in one hand, wet rag in the other and blob of raw eggs in the middle. "I dropped the carton."

The clock on the wall said it was only 5:30 a.m. "Where's Aunt Eileen?"

"Sick." Sean flipped a bacon strip. "Making her breakfast."

Finn laughed. "Or trying."

Allison looked to Ethan fidgeting with the coffeepot. "Hasn't she ever been sick before?"

All three heads turned and looked at Allison as though she'd just declared the moon was indeed made of green cheese. "No," they echoed.

Not the homemaker that Aunt Eileen was, Allison was smart enough to know few ailments handled fried bacon well. "What kind of sick?"

Again three heads turned, then one by one each Farraday man shrugged.

"Okay. I think I'd better go see for myself. Be right back."

"First room on the left," Sean called out to her as she climbed the stairs.

"Left," she mumbled, and turned at the first door. "Hello there."

Propped atop a hundred pillows covered with bulky feather comforters, Aunt Eileen reminded Allison of a scene from a movie about the first Queen Elizabeth. "Don't come too close, I might be contagious."

Allison stopped in her tracks though she doubted, if she hadn't contracted dengue or some other jungle fever by now, that whatever Aunt Eileen had would be a problem. "How do you feel?"

"Lousy." Aunt Eileen gave two soft dry coughs.

"Doesn't sound like you're congested."

"Oh, no." She ran her fingers under her eyes from her nose across her cheeks. "I can feel the pressure all in here."

"I see." Allison inched closer. "Do you have a fever?"

"101. I took some aspirin. I'm sure it's just a twenty-four hour thing I must have picked up in town yesterday. A good day of rest and fluids and I'll be fine."

The woman was right, rest, take two aspirin and drink plenty of fluids was as good of medical advice as she could have given. "Are you hungry?"

"Not really." Eileen's nose scrunched with distaste. "Maybe some nice tea. Chamomile."

Allison nodded. "I'll see that you get some."

"Oh." Aunt Eileen held up her hand. "I'm sorry to put this on you, dear, but can you please see to it that the boys don't wreck the house while I'm not looking? I have a casserole in the freezer you can defrost. And of course, I'm so thankful you're here to help Ethan since I won't be able to be his legs for now."

"Yes." She did her best to offer a sincere smile.

Back in the kitchen, she surveyed the situation. The fridge was stocked, the pantry was the size of a small apartment, and the freezer had more than one casserole. Too bad Allison didn't have a clue which casserole Eileen had meant. From where she stood Allison could see into the laundry room and the growing pile of

ETHAN   133

dirty clothes the family caregiver had not gotten to.

The sun was beginning to light the morning sky. She'd been in the house long enough to know the normal routine was breakfast, then saddling the horses and ready for the day's work at first light.

Tightening the sash on her robe, Allison turned to Finn, still mopping the floor. "Let me have that. You guys go get the horses ready. I'll pack up a couple of egg sandwiches for you to take."

"You don't have to do that."

Allison smiled. "No I don't, but I want to." And much to her surprise, though she'd never considered herself the domestic type, she really did.

Finn and his father nodded and, grabbing their hats from the hook by the door, made their way outside to the barn.

Ethan turned to her. "What can I do?"

"Stay out of my way." She laughed. "You can wait for Brittany to wake, I'm going to make breakfast." Rolling up her sleeves she sucked in a breath and reached for the fridge and another carton of eggs. The way her life had taken a new turn, waiting another day to go home wouldn't be the worst thing to happen by a long shot.

• • • •

"Four days. Aunt Eileen's never been sick for four days. And missing a Saturday poker game?" Wiggling his toes, Ethan relished the freedom of a cast-free foot and calculated how long it would take to get his calf muscle back in shape. His leg looked like it belonged to a 90-pound weakling.

"She is getting older." Brooks checked the pulse in Ethan's ankle.

"Not that old."

Brooks slid his hand up to Ethan's knee to check another pulse. "Any word on Fancy?"

Ethan shook his head.

"What about the judge?"

"Yes, thank heaven. We're on the docket for Monday. Allison signed an affidavit for me."

"Good." Brooks patted his brother's leg. "The foot too. Let me take a look at the x-rays and we'll see if you need another cast or if we can put you in a boot."

Ethan was hoping for a boot. The damn cast had been a pain in the neck for walking, standing, bathing, and just about life all around. At least he could take the boot off and enjoy a normal shower.

"So what's the prognosis?" DJ stood in the doorway to the exam room.

"Don't know yet."

DJ hefted one shoulder in a what-can-you-do gesture. "Saw the truck out front. Was about to call you so I stopped by instead."

"Any word on Fancy?"

DJ shook his head. "It's like she fell off the face of the earth. Again."

"Yeah, again. From what Allison says she's good at that."

"How are things going?" DJ moved closer to the exam table.

"Allison?"

His brother rolled his eyes. "Yes, Allison."

"What's to go? She's helping with the house and the baby and as soon as Aunt Eileen is back on her feet Allison is going home to California."

"And you're okay with that?"

"Of course I'm okay with that." At least that's what he'd kept telling himself, but with each passing day he wasn't so sure he believed himself any more.

"All right." Brooks entered the room and smiled at DJ. "Hey, anything new to report?"

DJ shook his head. "Nope."

"Okay." Brooks turned to Ethan. "You're going to like this. Bone is nicely healed. Honestly, it looks better than I would have expected for almost exactly six weeks."

"I got good genes." Ethan grinned.

"Yeah, well. Even so. You still have a great deal of soft tissue damage." He slapped the x-ray on a backlit block. "See all this gray stuff?"

Ethan and DJ nodded.

"That's not supposed to be there."

Lucky him. "So now what?"

"I can prescribe the boot. Once the soft tissue improves your orthopedist will probably want you to start physical therapy. Any idea yet if you'll be able to do that around here or if you have to return to Pendleton?"

"No. Nothing for sure yet." Though he was pretty confident with his hand still numb, going back to home station was not going to be a priority.

"All right then. We've got some orthotics in the storeroom gearing up for the new clinic. I think we'll have one just about your size."

Ethan's grin pulled at his cheeks and his mood. With all the stress of the last few weeks, finally getting out of that damn cast was better than sex. Well, maybe.

● ● ● ●

Catherine had brought her daughter Stacy over to visit with Aunt Eileen and the baby. The little girl adored being with the real life doll. The interaction made Allison wonder if her sister had been that excited to be around her when she was a baby.

"She doesn't look that sick to me." Catherine took another sip of coffee.

"I think she's feeling much better but enjoying all the attention." Allison had never thought Aunt Eileen was that sick to begin with, but figured after twenty-five years of raising this brood, she deserved a few days of bed rest.

"How about you? Holding up okay?"

"Oh yeah. I've learned to appreciate the simple pleasures in life. A soft bed and hot running water."

Catherine laughed. "Can't get much simpler than that. Listen, tonight is girls' night. A few of us are getting together at Becky's place over the animal clinic to watch movies and drink margaritas. Care to join us?"

"Oh, I don't know."

"The guys can handle Stacy and Brittany."

"I'm sure they can. It's not that."

"Then what?"

Allison was at a loss for words. How could she tell a beautiful woman like Catherine who had probably been prom and homecoming queen that girls' night was a new concept for Allison. Work hard and work harder had been her unspoken mantra. "Then nothing. Thank you for including me."

"Don't think twice. It's a little startling to have spent most of your life working eighty hours a week in a bustling city and then one day find yourself in the middle of West Texas ranch country."

"Try working seventy-two hours straight with only a cot and a nap in the bustling city only to find yourself in a raft floating down the Amazon."

"You got me on that one." Catherine stood to refill her cup. "Want another?"

Allison shook her head. "Don't you get a little bored with this slower paced life?"

"It's not really as slow as you might think. Ranch work starts before sunup. Connor is working on building his own stable but until the wedding he's still living here and working the ranch with his brothers."

"Yeah, I noticed. Thought it was kind of nice."

"Don't get us wrong. We're not that tied to traditional conventions, but with Stacy so young…" Catherine shrugged and Allison grinned.

There hadn't been any doubt in her mind that she'd made the right choice not fighting for full time custody of Brittany. Still, every day, every new thing she learned about the people in this family only reassured her that if there was a chance in hell of Brittany having a charmed life, it would be here in Farraday country.

"Anyhow," Catherine retook her seat, "I've been keeping pretty busy setting up the legal side of the new stable. It also turns out that there are quite a few folks in town who are thrilled not to have to drive to Butler Springs for decent legal advice. Though making wills and settling small claims disputes isn't high profile, getting a chance to help people like Charlotte and Jake Thomas creates a nice balance." She took a sip of the warm coffee. "And besides, I'm really having a blast setting up the new foundation."

"Foundation? For what?"

"Equine therapy."

"Really?" When Allison had been on track with neurology, she'd had some interest in the benefits of equine therapy on both children and adults post-op. "How is that?"

"Not many people are going to truck all the way out here for regular therapy, but I came across some articles on summer camps for handicapped kids that use horses for therapy. Connor and I both loved the idea."

"So you're starting a foundation for… underprivileged children?"

Catherine tapped her nose. "Spot on. We really are loving it. There's something enormously satisfying about helping those who can't do for themselves that a corporate courtroom win can't beat."

"You're preaching to the choir."

"What choir?" Ethan hobbled into the room and Allison's gaze dropped to his foot.

"They fitted you with a walking boot?"

"Yes, ma'am."

Allison wasn't sure if she'd ever seen Ethan grin quite so wide. "They did tell you not to abuse it. You still need to stay off your feet and keep that leg elevated."

"Yes, doctor. But you'll be happy to know that Dr. Brooks was very clear on my instructions and that abuse of privileges could set me back."

"Okay. Then sit down. That's an order."

She'd been wrong. His grin got even wider. The last few days, with mostly only the two of them home all day long except for mealtime and after supper, an easy rapport had settled between them—once she'd gotten over her embarrassment at kissing him,

"Oh crap." Catherine looked at her phone then up at the kitchen clock. "How did I miss what time it is? I've gotta run. I told Connor I'd leave him supper before girls' night." She sprang from her seat, leaned against Ethan and planted a kiss on his cheek. "Glad to see you up and mobile."

"Me too," he smiled down at his future sister-in-law.

"Okay munchkin, let's boogie." Catherine stuck her hand out to her daughter.

"Do we have to?" Despite the question, the little girl was already on her feet and accepting the proffered hand.

"Yes, we have to." Almost out the door, Catherine called over her shoulder, "Don't do anything I wouldn't do." And then the door closed behind her and Stacy.

"Come on." Allison stood, moved to where Ethan was and pulled out the chair. "Sit."

Ethan plopped heavily in the large wooden chair.

"And foot up." She slid the nearby chair under his foot. "And—"

"Bend my knee, yes, I got that one." He smiled at her and the twinkle in his eyes made her want to smile back at him.

"All right. What would you like to drink? Cola, tea, water?"

"Nothing right now." He reached out and snatched her hand in his with a gentle tug. Allison landed in his lap with a squeal.

"Ethan."

"Sit," he repeated in the same tone she'd used on him earlier. "You won't let me stand and I have something I want to say."

All she could do was nod. The nearness of so much of him had her feeling like a giddy teen—even if she herself had never been anything close to giddy before.

"Every time I think about how you just stepped into a crazy household that isn't your responsibility—"

"It's not crazy, believe me."

"Okay, busy, is that better?" He smiled again.

"I can accept busy." This time she didn't stop herself from smiling back.

"Good. How you stepped into this busy household that isn't your responsibility and kept us all from starving—"

"All I did was heat up a few casseroles your aunt made, and I have it on good authority that said aunt has taught all of you how to cook."

"Yeah, but you saw us that first morning. We might know how to fend for ourselves, but we don't do as well with crowds."

She chuckled at the memory. "You guys did look a little bewildered."

"Would you please let a man say thank you?" Exasperation clung to his words.

"I'm sorry." Her voice came out low and meek.

His gaze latched onto hers. "You really are beautiful inside and out, Beatrice Allison Monroe." His finger reached up and ran down the tip of her nose. "Just accept the compliment and say thank you."

Allison swallowed hard. That was twice he'd told her she was beautiful. She wasn't quite sure if she'd eased forward or he leaned in her direction, but by the time the word *you* had followed *thank*, her lips were against his and her arm had snaked around his neck.

"Oh, Allison," he mumbled against her lips seconds before pulling her tight against him and plundering her mouth, sending spikes of electricity shooting to every nerve ending.

"Allison." The back door slammed open and Connor stormed inside, Sean on his heels.

"What's wrong?" She scurried up from Ethan's lap, only the panic in the two men's eyes staving off the mortification that now coursed through her. "Oh, God. Catherine—"

"No. She and Stacey are fine," Connor said hurriedly. "DJ

just called. There's been an accident."

Ethan stood up and positioned himself behind her, his strong hands on her shoulders.

"Youth group coming home from a church outing. The driver blacked out, the van sped up and then flipped off the road."

Allison was already moving to her room, wishing she'd brought a full medical bag. "Any other injuries?"

"We don't know. The Brady boy used the driver's cell phone to call for help. Esther said kids were screaming and shouting and the Brady kid was trying to keep them calm and talk to Esther at the same time."

"Is Brooks on his way?" Allison asked.

"Yes, but they're coming from the opposite direction of town."

"How far out are the kids?" Ethan asked.

The head of the family looked to his son. "There's the other problem."

Ethan's spine straightened.

"None of the kids know. They think they left the ghost town maybe twenty minutes ago but one of the ground rules for the retreat was no electronics. Not a single kid has a cell phone on them. They could have been on the road for twenty minutes or an hour. And we're not even sure which route the driver took."

"Shit," Ethan mumbled.

Allison tossed scissors and clean kitchen towels into a bag. In the jungle she could be out the door in five, here she might need ten. "I'll need all the first aid supplies you've got in the house. Bandages, antiseptic. If you've got some splints you use for the animals, I'll take them. We may have people in shock. I'll need blankets."

"On my way." Sean tore off for the stairs. "I'll get you a pair of boots too. You look to be about the same size as Grace."

"Boots?"

Connor shrugged apologetically. "Rattlesnakes."

Oh Lord. She nearly cringed at the thought. This was one

more thing she was *not* going to let herself worry about. Supplies. She needed to gather supplies. She'd probably need backboards, neck braces...Blast. "Better bring towels and duct tape if you have it. We may need to stabilize some injuries."

"It might be too late, but we have a defibrillator in the barn." Connor was already moving to the back door. "I'll bring back some supplies for doctoring the horses. Adam always said people and animals aren't all that different."

"Connor," Ethan called, his voice like ice.

Connor grabbed the side of the doorjamb and skidded to a halt. "Yeah?"

"How long since anyone's taken the helicopter up?"

"Last month. Jed Carrington came in and helped us locate some lost steers." He glanced down at his brother's boot. "You up to it?"

"Ethan, no." Loading ice into a cooler, Allison froze.

He didn't respond to her. "I'll take it up, report back with coordinates. If we need to evac the driver to the hospital, the helo will be the fastest way."

"Surely there's an air ambulance service at the nearest hospital?" Allison understood why Ethan wanted to help, but still...

Connor nodded. "Once they're notified we need them, the hospital is forty-five minutes away as the crow flies."

CHAPTER NINETEEN

In order to operate the helo Ethan had to remove the boot. When Allison found out, he had a feeling she was going to kill him. Thinking of possible ways to distract her was the only thing that helped him ignore that his leg now hurt like a son of a bitch.

He'd been in the air almost twenty minutes when he spotted the van and radioed his brother. "We're in luck."

"Where are they?" Connor responded. He and Catherine and Sean had all taken a truck to help transport the children back to town. Allison was in Connor's truck.

"Off FM 3610. What's your location now?"

"Coming up on 3610 in about two clicks."

"You should be less than twenty minutes out. Clock your speedometer. In about twenty miles, look for fresh skid marks to the left. The van's hidden by a crop of mesquite."

"Mesquite?"

"Yeah. I'm going to put this bird down and see what the damage is. See you in twenty."

"Fifteen."

Ethan almost laughed. If anyone could put the pedal to the metal and shave the most time off a run, it was him or Connor. He certainly hoped Allison had a little race driver in her blood.

Willing his bad leg to do as his mind instructed, Ethan set the bird on the ground with a bit less grace than he would have liked. Leaving the helo set for a quick start, he strapped the boot on and hopped out, landing mostly on his good foot. Mostly.

He'd disregarded doctor's orders flying out, no point in being careful now. Doing the closest thing to running possible with a non-flex orthopedic boot on, Ethan dashed to the crash site. On his left a handful of young teens huddled near the mesquite. "Everyone all right here?" He slowed but didn't stop.

A few voices said yes, a couple of heads nodded, and Ethan kept moving.

From the looks of it the van had dipped into a drainage ditch at full speed and momentum pitched it over a few times away from the road. Closer, he braced himself. A man didn't make it through years in the Marine Corps without losing his share of buddies, but nothing prepared someone for dealing with injured—or worse—children.

"Mr. Farraday." A boy who Ethan figured had to be the Brady kid since he looked just like his dad, held one arm against his ribs, flagged him to the driver then returned that hand to the driver's head.

The kid had taken off his t-shirt and was applying pressure to a gash on the man's forehead. Ethan was no expert, but he knew head wounds bled like old faithful and figured this kid had things under control. Except… "What happened to your arm?"

"Bumped it." He shrugged, then winced. "I didn't want to move him. He hasn't come to, but he is breathing."

Ethan put his finger to the guy's carotid and blew out a sigh of relief. Weak but, yeah, the guy was still breathing.

"I also found a small bottle of aspirin in his pocket. I figured he must have a bad heart so I put one under his tongue. He almost bit me."

How old was this kid? Ethan was impressed. "Smart move, son. What else do we have here?" Ethan mumbled to no one in particular.

Another gal who he thought might be a Rankin, yelled to him. "Sarah Sue is trapped. We tried moving the seat but it won't budge."

Ethan surveyed the situation. "How are you doing, sweetie?"

"My foot hurts." The poor kid's voice cracked. She was trying so hard to be brave and not cry.

"I bet it does. We'll have you out of here in a minute." A

crowbar and brute force would do the trick. He didn't like what he saw next. At the back, a huddle of kids, a couple of puddles of blood, and sobs.

"Anybody home?" Allison's voice sounded behind him and not a moment too soon.

"Over here, Doc."

Her eyes widened a split second before she cut her way across the van, pausing only one second to check the driver's pulse as he had. He hadn't really given it any thought, but before now he'd never called her anything but her given name.

He reached the children about the same time as Allison did with the same alarm in her eyes as his must have had.

"Debbie's not waking up," a fragile blonde said through a sob, and Ethan's heart stuttered to a near stop.

Another older teen said, "She's not dead. But she groaned and tried to move so we've been holding her in place."

At first Ethan didn't quite understand the concern and then he saw it. A piece of metal long and sharp enough to do some serious damage protruded from the girl's side.

"I remembered from a TV show when I was a kid…"

A kid? What was he now?

"…Not to pull a lodged sharp object out because it might be acting as a plug. Was I right?"

Allison ran her hand across the worried teen's brow and brushed a loose lock of hair away from his face. "You absolutely did the right thing in not pulling it out *and* not letting her move."

Ethan looked back at the girl trapped under the seat. "I need to get a crowbar."

Allison nodded and opened her bag. "Why don't you take the kids who don't need treatment with you?"

"I don't want to leave my sister," the frightened girl whined.

"Me too?" The other teen helping with Debbie asked at the same time.

"No," Allison addressed her first. "I need you and your friend to continue to make sure Debbie doesn't move until I can get a backboard and strap her down."

The first young man's chest puffed slightly with pride, though the worry was still deep set in his eyes.

"Why don't you come help me find a crowbar for Sarah Sue?" He held his hand out to the young girl, who didn't budge. She seemed quite a bit younger than the other kids. "And when we get you back to town I'll have Miss Abbie give you a double scoop of chocolate ice cream for helping."

The child looked to her sister and bit on her trembling lower lip.

"She's going to be okay," Allison reassured the little girl. "It's okay for you to go help Mr. Farraday."

Ethan wondered how he'd gotten that wrong. How stupid to think the kid cared more about ice cream than her sister. To his surprise her small hand slipped into his. "I'm going to pick you up," he said, "it will be easier to get you out of here."

The little girl nodded and Ethan didn't miss the concern on Allison's face as her glance dropped briefly to his boot and then shifted to where she was seriously needed. He was almost out the door when Allison called back to him. "Tell Brooks to step on it, and have DJ order that air lift. Now."

Ethan nodded. Shifting the little girl onto one arm as though she were as light as Brittany, he used his free hand to call DJ. The medivac ordered, he continued to where the others were gathered. All the kids had a blanket and a bottle of water and Connor and Catherine were putting ice on sprains and cleaning small cuts and bruises.

His father came walking toward him from his truck carrying a three foot flat bar and bolt cutter. "I got a look inside while you and Allison were dealing with the kids in the back. Is the young girl going to be okay?"

Ethan nodded. He hoped Allison wasn't just saying pretty words to the little sister.

"Let's get Sara Sue out. From the way that foot's swelling, the sooner the better."

By the time they'd broken Sarah Sue free, Brooks had arrived in his suburban, the closest thing to a country ambulance. He'd put the driver on oxygen and an IV and then together he and Allison maneuvered the still unconscious girl onto a backboard and strapped her in.

The look of sheer anguish on Allison's face as the airlift EMTs loaded the young teen onto the helo tore at something deep inside Ethan. Over the past week he'd learned more about her life, how hard she worked, and how much she cared. He didn't like the idea of her going home to California and him not being there for her. Of her working herself to death for the sake of a patient and then going home exhausted and drained to an empty house. Or worse, to give her all and lose a patient only to bear the pain alone in silence.

"Good thing the hospital dispatched the airlift as soon as we put them on standby." Brooks brushed his hands and looked to the second helo landing across the street. "This guy's lucky we could get an Air Evac from another hospital here this fast. I don't think he'd have lasted the drive."

"What I want to know," Connor rolled his neck, "is how the hell did that mesquite get all the way out here?"

Sean Farraday shook his head. "Someone's crazy grandmother probably got the bright idea to plant the thing by the side of the road."

"Oh yeah," Ethan chuckled. "Like that's going to shade West Texas."

His dad shook his head and walked away mumbling, "Crazy grandmothers."

A few of the parents who lived closer to the accident location than to town drove out to pick up their kids. The ones with cuts, bruises, sprains, or like the Brady kid who had broken his arm trying to get the driver's dead weight foot off the gas and press the brakes, were being transported back to town for Brooks to treat properly. Since the kids fit in the Suburban and the squad car, the rest of the Farradays were heading home.

Allison turned to face him. "I wish you didn't have to fly that thing home again."

"No problem. It's what I do." Or did.

"How much does it hurt?" She pointed to his foot with her chin.

He considered lying. "On a scale of one to ten? Eleven."

"Yeah, that's what I thought. But without you we wouldn't have known which road to take."

"The important thing is it all turned out well."

Connor trotted up beside them. "You coming with me or riding back with Ethan?"

"Go with Connor. Someone has to keep him from drag racing. The cops are pissy about that sort of thing."

Connor rolled his eyes. "Good thing for you we're in mixed company."

"Actually," Allison lifted her gaze to meet his, "I'm not sure I'm up to my first helicopter ride tonight."

Ethan nodded and resisted the temptation to pull her into his arms and beg her to stay. He was totally crazy. A gazillion women who would throw themselves at his feet to play Mrs. Farraday and he had to fall in love with this woman. And wasn't that a laugh and a half. Ethan Farraday in love.

• • • •

Holding her eyes open seemed like a monumental challenge. Not unusual after the adrenaline rush of emergency medicine. Either Allison was so wound up there was no coming down or, like a spinning top, she went full speed ahead one second and flopped over at a full stop the next.

"We're almost home." Connor pointed to the tiny glimmer of light in the distance.

Allison blinked. "How did that happen?"

"You fell asleep."

"Oh." She pushed herself more upright. "Sorry."

"Don't be. You needed the rest. You did good."

"I didn't do much."

"More than you think. Had any one of us, or some passerby, arrived first, they might have done the wrong thing by that girl."

That was true. Most people's instinct was to remove the offensive object and if proper medical care wasn't handy, the patient could easily bleed out. "Do you think Ethan's back yet?"

"Oh yeah. The helicopter goes twice as fast as a car and I'm not booking it."

Connor led the parade of trucks into the long Farraday drive. One by one they all exited the vehicles and dragged themselves into the house.

"Mommy," Stacy came running at Catherine and practically flew into her arms.

"Did you have a good time with Aunt Eileen?"

"And the baby too." Stacy beamed at her mother. "Can we have one of our own?"

Connor coughed, and Catherine smiled. "We'll have to think about it, dear."

The little girl frowned. "That's the same as no."

"Not necessarily." Connor got down on his haunches, and tucked the little girl into his shoulder. "After the wedding your mommy and I can...discuss it." Connor's smile lifted at one side in a cheeky grin and immediately Catherine's face brightened.

Is that what all women in love looked like? She'd seen that same beam of happiness in Meg and Toni and Becky. Did she light up like the proverbial Christmas tree whenever Ethan flashed her a sexy grin or said something nice?

"Are you okay, dear?" Aunt Eileen, obviously fully recovered, crossed the room to her. "You look suddenly pale."

Did she? And why not. Didn't everyone turn just a little green at the gills the first time they realized they'd fallen head over heels in love?

"I see you're feeling better." Sean came in behind the others.

"Yes." Eileen hesitated for a second. "A woman can only

handle so much time in bed."

Sean nodded and walked past the crowd in the doorway. "You young folks can keep talking, but I'm going to bed. Goodnight."

A round of goodnights filled the foyer, but one person was missing. And then she spotted him off to the right in the den. In his recliner, his ankle up, the boot off and a load of ice packing it on either side. *Stubborn goat.*

"I'm heading home too." Catherine turned toward the door. "Goodnight everyone."

Connor put a hand at the small of her back. "I'll give you a lift."

"Tonight, I'm not arguing." She kissed him lightly on the lips and, still carrying her daughter, trudged to the truck.

"Well." Aunt Eileen looked around, her gaze settling on Ethan and then to Allison and back. "It has been a long day. I'm turning in. Brittany just went down so you should probably do the same. Night."

Allison waved and Ethan winked. Apparently that was a family thing between those two because Eileen rolled her eyes and blew him a kiss.

Eileen was almost all the way up the stairs before Allison found the strength to put one foot in front of the other and join Ethan in the living room. "How bad is it?"

"Could be worse."

She couldn't argue with that. Making it all the way to the sofa at Ethan's side, she plopped down with absolutely no ladylike decorum. "My aunt is probably getting shivers."

"Why is that?"

"She can't roll over in her grave, she's not dead."

"Where is she?"

"England. She moved back when I started Stanford, but I like to think anytime I do something contrary to her British sensibilities she feels it."

"A little leftover teenage rebellion."

"Not leftover. It's all I've ever had."

With her eyes closed, she heard Ethan shifting in his chair, the ice fall to the side and then felt the sinking of the cushion beside her.

"I've been thinking." He turned her slightly, then his hands came down on her shoulders and his fingers began kneading.

"Oh my. I'll give you exactly two hours to stop doing that." She could so get used to this. "You were saying?"

"I may not be able to fly helicopters for Uncle Sam anymore, but I can still fly civilian helos."

Allison made an extreme effort to nod her head.

"And I can do that near San Francisco as easily as Texas."

Had she heard that right? Glancing at him over her shoulder she blinked. "Say again?"

"Brittany might like living driving distance to the beach."

Allison swung completely around and faced him.

"I know housing in California is pretty expensive, but I have some money saved and—"

Placing her finger on his lips, she cut him off. "You're willing to move to California?"

He nodded. "Or the Amazon if that's what you want."

"To… be … near me?"

Again his head bobbed.

Her finger fell and her mouth dropped slightly open.

"Why is that so hard to believe?"

"I, uhm…"

"Love you and want to be with you."

She had no idea if he was speaking *to* her or *for* her but her mouth fell open again. This time pretty wide open.

Ethan chuckled. And she snapped her mouth shut.

"You know," he continued to smile, "a man could get a complex if you keep looking at him likes he's speaking Martian. I love you Allison, I don't want to lose you."

The size of the grin pulling at her cheeks matched the swell in her heart. "What a coincidence because it just so happens, Ethan Farraday, that I love you."

"You do?" Now his voice seemed a little incredulous.

"Very much." She nodded. "And your whole family, and your friends, and the fresh air, and Sunday suppers, and people caring more about each other than themselves. I love the idea of helping build an A-class health facility so people don't have to travel a hundred miles for treatment. I love the balance of work, life and family." She hung her arms around his neck. "I love you, and, I don't want Brittany to grow up in California."

His eyes twinkled bright. "You don't?"

"No." She drew closer to him. "I don't. And by the way."

"Yes?"

"Did Connor get a chance to mention how we found the crash site?"

Ethan shook his head.

"Between the ditch and the grass and that tree, there was no way to see the van from the road. And the skid marks weren't very dark or long."

"The Brady boy wasn't in a place to really slow the van down. So how did you find it?"

"A gray dog came running out of nowhere barking."

"Dog?"

"Gray."

"I didn't see a dog."

"Yeah, well. Apparently that's how it works. So according to your aunt's matchmaking dog theory, we don't have any choice but to wind up happily together."

Ethan's lips hovered over hers. "Then by all means, let's tell my aunt about the dog."

EPILOGUE

"Ya think folks may be getting tired of Farraday weddings?" Finn took a sip of champagne and wondered why this stuff was so popular for making toasts.

"Nah." Ethan downed a swallow of his favorite longneck beer. "Folks love any excuse for a good party that comes with free food and drink and a sappy romance to boot."

"Uh, oh." Finn shifted in front of his brother. "You'd better sit quick."

Immediately Ethan dropped into the seat beside him. "Did she see me?"

"Don't think so." Finn spied Ethan's fiancée cutting across the dance floor. She looked to be a woman on a mission.

Ethan tracked the room, his gaze landing on Allison's approach. For all his bluster, at the first sight of the woman he totally lit up like a Texas night on the fourth of July. Ever since the van accident a few weeks ago, the two had been inseparable. Together, Ethan and Allison met with the judge who granted the termination of Francine's parental rights. When Ethan had to report to an orthopedist for follow up on his leg, Allison had gone with him. When she flew home to San Francisco to take care of business, Ethan and Brittany had gone too. Finn had no idea who would tie the knot next, Declan or Ethan, but he hoped they'd give him and the town a chance to recoup before having to buy more wedding presents.

"Don't you dare stand up," Allison said to Ethan from several feet away. "You know what the doctor said. No more than twenty minutes at a time on your feet and then elevated for at least an hour. You're way over your limit for the day already." Allison reached Ethan as the last words rolled off her lips. Lips she used to sweetly kiss Ethan with just enough feeling to have Finn checking out the shine on his boots.

A lightweight hand came to rest around Finn's middle. His cousin, Hannah Farraday, the youngest female in the family, gave Finn a squeeze and peck on the cheek. "I don't know who's cuter, the bride and groom or those two."

Finn turned, pleased with the chance to visit with one of the Austin clan. Since they'd all grown up and stopped spending summers together, he didn't see enough of any of them. "Wait till Sunday supper tomorrow, it'll feel like a regular love fest."

"Which would explain why Mom and Aunt Eileen are taking bets on who's going to be next." His cousin chuckled. "Listening to them talk about dogs and fate and destiny, I've never been so happy to live in Dallas."

"Oh yeah. I bet." He smiled at the cute way she wrinkled her nose. Less than a year younger than Grace, she had spent more time with the West Texas Farradays over summers and school breaks than any of the cousins. "So you're adapting to the big D?" he asked.

Hannah shrugged. "I'm a little south of Dallas proper so it's not as claustrophobic as it could be."

A few piano notes sounded and Hannah's eyes opened wide. "Oh no. Tell me Connor and Catherine hired a DJ *and* a band."

"I don't think so."

Across the room, Connor and his bride looked up. Adam had been sitting at a nearby table and pushed to his feet.

"Where did they get a piano?" Ethan asked while standing, despite Allison's insistence he stay seated.

Several more notes played followed by the familiar words, "The moment I wake up…"

"Never mind the piano," Finn said, "who gave them a microphone?"

"Them?" Allison asked.

The second line of the familiar tune "Say A Little Prayer" was sung by a more powerful voice.

"Oh," Allison looked around for the piano. "They're good."

Hannah groaned. "They must have been talking about *My Best Friend's Wedding* again. Every time they have a glass of wine at a wedding and someone doesn't hide the piano, we wind up with a serenade."

Another verse belted out, stronger, louder, and Finn spotted his two aunts sharing a mic as expected. What he hadn't anticipated was seeing Meg to one side of the older women singing along, with Grace and Becky on their other side doing a darn good impression of the Supremes. Or was it the Spinners? To his right, the sound of rhythmic clapping startled him. Not the clapping itself, but that it had come from Allison.

She shrugged. "I can't carry a tune."

By the time the words "forever and ever" came along, Catherine and Toni were huddled around Meg and Finn's aunts singing loudly.

"Well, maybe I can just hum a little." Allison patted Ethan on the shoulder and scurried across the floor to join her future in-laws.

"Dear Lord," Hannah muttered.

"What?" Finn and Ethan echoed.

"I think," she waved an arm in the general direction of the two women hamming it up for the crowd with their entourage of backup singers, "Mom and Aunt Eileen have found their people."

"Well, you know what they say," Ethan shifted his weight and eased forward a step. "If you can't beat 'em, join 'em."

By the end of the song, everyone in the place was either singing, clapping, or channeling 1960s girl groups. Finn had to laugh. He loved his family. All of them. He even loved his aunt Eileen's crazy poker playing club. But the last few months had brought way more drama and excitement than he was used to. It was time for some old-fashioned peace and quiet. No matter what bets his aunts made, he wasn't worried about a disappearing dog, or fate, or destiny, or an-on-your-doorstep mate. Nope. All this dog talk was pure hogwash. When he was ready to marry, he'd pick his own wife, one who was simple, uncomplicated, and most especially—drama free.

Enjoy an excerpt from

Finn

"**M**an that feels good." Finn set his hat by his side, leaned against the post, and lifted his face to the sun.

"Move went pretty quick this morning." Finn's dad, Sean Farraday, slapped his hat against his thigh and looked across the pasture at the contented cows, drinking and snacking and pretty much doing what cows do all year long. "Mothering up went well, too."

"Yep." A couple of mother cows were still looking for their calf, but not as many had been separated on route to this pasture as in days past. So far the few that seemed hell bent on going back where they came from were being held behind the invisible line in the grass the dogs had drawn. Scratching the dust from his hair Finn put his hat back on and listened to the steady thrum of cows calling out for their calves, or perhaps simply chewing the fat with their friends.

The best part of saddling up in the pitch black of early morning to start moving cows at first light was the chance to relax and watch Mother Nature at work until lunchtime. "Flow seems off on the water. I'll pull the pump tomorrow before we start working on the new fence section."

Sean nodded and sat beside his son. "Some days, I look out at the pasture and I'd swear I can see you and your brothers roping the dummy, or playing with the water, or even just worn out and napping."

A smile took over Finn's face. He remembered those days well. Especially when they wound up in pastures by the creek. Those were fun times swimming, catching toads, and all around doing his best to keep up with his older brothers.

"Gates closed. So far none of the herd is backtracking." Sam their ranch hand left his horse ground tied with the others and came up beside his bosses. "Are we taking turns heading back to the house for lunch?"

Shaking his head, Finn pulled a blade of grass from the ground. "Nope. Aunt Eileen is bringing lunch today."

"Sweet." Sam peeled off his gloves and shoved them in his back pocket.

Finn pushed to his feet, noticing a couple spots in the fence that would need to be fixed in the days to come. "She has been doting on Ethan and the baby."

"Speaking of which." Sean Farraday stood up beside his son and ranch hand, all three eyeing the large ranch truck making its way across the pasture. The men smiled like fools when the door opened and out popped Aunt Eileen.

"Y'all made good time this morning." She slammed the door shut with her foot.

"No water to cross. Calves kept up pretty good." Sam moved to reach for the aluminum tray. "Allow me."

As they'd done for ages and eons, the trays of warm food were spread out on the tail of the truck and one by one, Sean first, plates were filled and folks moved to sit and enjoy.

"Boy, I missed these hot lunches," Sam said.

Frowning, Eileen looked up from her plate. "It's not like you don't have a freezer stocked with my casseroles."

"Gotta admit, it's nice to have a warm meal midday to fill the belly." Finn kissed his aunt on the cheek and turned to where the others sat.

"Hmm," Aunt Eileen groused, plate in hand, leaning against the truck. "Not my fault you two are still single."

"Now don't get your britches in a knot." Sean shook his head. "Sam and Finn didn't mean anything more than we just appreciate a hearty lunch is all. Thank you."

"Yes, ma'am, Miss Eileen," Sam repeated. "No matter who I marry, she'll have a hard time competing with your cooking."

Just a hint of pink singed his aunt's cheeks and Finn thought they really didn't pay her compliments nearly often enough. "Thanks, Aunt Eileen. This is delicious."

One of the dogs began barking and Sean turned, recognizing his dog King's bark. King was one of the best cattle dogs Finn had ever seen. The animal did the work of two men some days. Without the dogs they'd never be able to run all the cattle with just the three of them.

The louder lowing coming from the cows along with shifting by the animals near King, had Finn putting his plate on the tail of the truck and walking around to grab the rifle from the rack.

"You thinking the cows disturbed a rattler?" Aunt Eileen scanned the ground around the truck. "All these years and those things still give me the heebie jeebies."

"You're not the only one." Sam smiled at her. "Back in Wyoming, we could kill a snake with a shovel, but down here, the snakes are bigger than the shovels."

The closer Finn got to where all the ruckus was, the less of the snake jokes being told by the truck he could hear. Sam was a nice guy, he'd come to Texas a few years ago during the rodeo circuit complaining about Wyoming being cold enough to freeze a cow to the ground where it stood. After a couple of days talking and drinking, the Farradays had a new ranch hand. First time anyone not a blood relative lived or worked on the ranch, and Sam hadn't yet done anything to make Finn or his dad regret the decision.

"Yep," Finn mumbled to himself. Not quite upon the bedlam, like a pair of Latin maracas at an all night party, the snake's rattle could be heard loud and clear. Good at their jobs, giving the rattler a wide berth, King and Bo had the few cows too indifferent to do more than give the snake a dirty look, moving away from striking distance. Truth was around this part of the country more dogs than cows got bit by snakes, and the last thing Finn wanted was for either of the dogs to get bitten.

"That'll do, Bo. That'll do, King." Like the well-trained cattle dogs they were, the two quit and hurried to Finn's side. At least real life wasn't like an old cowboy movie. He'd be able to shoot the hissing thing from where he stood and the worst that would happen is a dirty-cow-look would be flashed in his direction. The stampede of cattle because of a gun shot in the distance was all Hollywood hooey.

Not wasting time, he brought up the rifle, took aim at the angry reptile, and fired. Still squirming and wiggling, like a fish out of water, the snake hit the ground hard.

His eyes on the intruder Finn called over his shoulder, "Hey Sam, bring me that shovel."

Shovel in hand, Sam ran up to him. "Nice shot!"

"Let's get his head chopped off and buried before one of the dogs tries to play with him and gets bit."

With a nod Sam took off a few feet to where the rattler had finally stopped moving.

Turning toward where his dad and aunt watched the excitement, Finn did a double take. Off in the distance a gray shadow streaked across the pasture. A suspiciously four legged furry shadow.

"Oh, man. Fourteen buttons on the tail." Sam shook his head. "This guy must have really made some noise. Just thinking about it makes my hair stand on end."

Finn nodded. He felt the same way, except the shiver going up his back didn't have a blessed thing to do with the rattler.

MEET CHRIS

USA TODAY Bestselling Author of more than a dozen contemporary novels, including the award winning *Champagne Sisterhood*, Chris Keniston lives in suburban Dallas with her husband, two human children, and two canine children. Though she loves her puppies equally, she admits being especially attached to her German Shepherd rescue. After all, even dogs deserve a happily ever after.

More on Chris and her books can be found at
www.chriskeniston.com

Follow Chris on Facebook at ChrisKenistonAuthor
or on Twitter @ckenistonauthor

Questions? Comments?
I would love to hear from you.
You can reach me at chris@chriskeniston.com

Manufactured by Amazon.ca
Bolton, ON

32044946R00099